STILL TIME

Short and Shorter Stories

Michael Cocchiarale

Fomite

Burlington, Vermont

This is a work of fiction. Names, characters, places and incidents are either the product of the author's imagination or are used fictiously. Any resemblance to actual persons, living or dead, events or locales is entirely coincidental.

ISBN-13: 978-1-937677-01-5
Library of Congress Control Number: 2011943865

Fomite
58 Peru Street
Burlington, VT 05401
www.fomitepress.com

Cover Photo: Lisa Cocchiarale
Author Photo: Lisa Cocchiarale

For Lisa

CONTENTS

ONE

Worse Things

What the hell are you doing? Put it back in there.

But there's green stuff on it.

Green what?

See?

Stop peeing first. And don't cry.

The boy moaned—a brave attempt at compromise.

You see everybody else, these *men*? They're watching you go on.

But look!

Will you stop peeing?

Yes.

A few dark patches of green clung to the underside of the boy's squiggly scrotum.

That's just some seaweed, the father said.

Seaweed? Seaweed? The boy began to hyperventilate.

The father turned around, opening his hands to the others. There's worse things. Right fellas?

A hairy backed man turned from the sink and tugged playfully at his crotch. I'll show him worse . . .

Hard laughter shot against the restroom walls.

The father winked and said, at least that means *you're* getting something.

More laughter, cracking like the ochre tiles on the wall.

Another man sighed, fish white stomach looming: Marriage will do that to you.

Murmurs of assent, chuckles sharp like splintered shells. The punch of soap dispensers. The rip and tear of paper towels. A sudden fart behind a graffitied door.

The boy stared at these men—all these strange, colossal faces, these squinty grins. As his father moved from the urinal, the boy started flapping his hands. Cartoon trunks dropped and died around his ankles.

What am I . . . going . . . ?

Christ, you always have to be a baby. The father raised his hand, brought it so close the boy could see the scrapes and gouges along that silver wedding band.

Last summer, things were so much better. His mother used to bring him in with her, and he got a stall all for himself. Are you done yet? she'd say after a nice, comfortable time. Sometimes he stood for awhile, staring at the raised up seat coming together like a claw. He'd think of father crackling a lobster in half, its dead legs scraping against the plate . . . father sucking out ghost colored meat with a big fat ugly kiss. Times like these, the water just wouldn't come. That's fine, Mom would say, her voice warm yet wavy like the parking lot by 10 am. You take your time now, dear. There's plenty of time for the sun.

All I Am Is Nine

In the dead grass by the street was a hole with broken pipes and dirty water. Small soldiers on the lump of dirt the men had scooped were climbing down to kill.

Stay back, Mom said from the porch. You're too close to the road. Something bad will happen.

Her arms were crossed. She looked like something bad already happened, like how she mostly looked before Dad would say, you take your pills? He'd put his hands up on his head and say, What we throwing money down the drain for if you're not?

Now, she said, slapping her gown. It looked like a sheet they pull over bodies on the news.

I marched my soldiers down the hill. They were closer to the sleeping enemies. Dirt and pebbles crumbled down on the plastic houses. Some people were by the windows, watching all the scary holes of the guns.

A big loud car made me look up at the street. I saw a flashing bumper, and a long black cat creeping. The cat froze. Mom screamed. The loud car drove over it, and . . . magic!—the cat came out again. But the scream kept going and the cat hopped like a frog or kangaroo, looking at me with different huge green forced out eyes.

Then the cat started coughing, like there was something in his throat and it turned out to be blood—blood and whatever else is red like guts. He jerked like a puppet, then just like that he didn't move at all. The mouth stayed open, like Mom when the phone rang and she said, that's bad news, I just know it.

The scream was gone and so was Mom. My soldiers stood on the hill, their guns were ready to shoot. They were waiting for me to say the word. The people in the houses were waiting to die.

The Darden twins came running. Andy clapped his hands and said, cool man look at that!

I ran inside the house and called Mom's name again and again. The sun suddenly went away and the living room was like a hole with furniture.

She was in the backroom, with no windows or TV. She was rocking in her broken chair, eyes running out of her face. Dad had hands on his head and said you stop this now or I'll take you back.

Oh you'd love that, wouldn't you? she said. You'd love to just put me in—

Dad raised a hand and said, Stop now or else.

I went away, back through the shadows of the house, outside into clouds. Jason Darden was poking the cat with a stick.

Put it down his mouth, Andy said.

Jason tapped the stick against its teeth. Open wide, he said.

Andy hit his brother. Put it in its butt. That's better!

I left my soldiers on the hill. I left the enemies in their houses, alive. I climbed into the hole. The men would be coming soon to work. Brown water came through the tiny eyes of my shoes.

Squeeze

Three days after buying the ten-speed, father slapped me hard—not in the face (after all, he had a public reputation to uphold) but on the outer thigh. The sound was loud, like a bad dive into a pool. From the porch swing next door, Jimmy Frain looked up, and our eyes locked like new bricks of Lego. I ran up into my room and threw myself into the space between the bed and wall. Moments later, father hovered outside the door I'd slammed.

"Three days and you let it get stolen," he said. "Do you think I'm going to just run out and get another?"

That afternoon, I'd been in the QuikPik for just two or three minutes, first searching through the freezer for a bomb pop, and then waiting out the girl ahead of me, who paid for a two-liter Coke in nickels that dribbled endlessly onto the counter. When I stepped out the door, some unidentifiable older and bigger boy was standing up on the pedals of my bike, wobbling toward the asphalt horizon. I stood frozen—partly from shock, partly from shame. Eventually I thawed, but fear of father froze me right back up again, colder than my popsicle perspiring in its wrapper.

"Of course," father continued. "I'll just go get another. Like it's an ice cream cone you dropped on the sidewalk." He opened the door then and stood on the other side of the bed, eyes scoring me with anger.

"I'm out . . . do you know how much? Do you?"

I put the edge of the blanket over my head.

"One hundred and fifty-nine dollars and ninety-nine cents. Do you know what that kind of money looks like? I'd count it out for you, but I'm a little short these days."

My head fell against the hard frame of the bed. I sobbed loudly, thoroughly, pouring out tears and sucking in snot. As I listened to his labored breathing slacken, I was lulled into thinking the worst might be over. Instead, father slapped the bed with his mitt-sized hands and hissed, "You'll goddamn pay for this." I shuddered at the open-ended nature of his threat, which suggested far more than the mere loss of allowance. I remembered last month, two doors down, when Mrs. Hall locked her husband out of the house one night, and he stood in unzipped work pants and his car carrier stomach, banging on the door and crying, "I'll kill you—I'll kill you all" until the police arrived to scurry him away. It made me faint to think about what people might be capable of when pushed past their own secret and arbitrary lines of resistance.

∗∗∗

Not long after Jimmy's father called him in for dinner—not long after the good boy's sing-song response reached through the bedroom window to tease my burning ears—I heard mom banging through the front door, returning from work with a bag of groceries. As a cashier at the Shop-a-Lot, she was on her feet all day, and the tired shuffle of her shoes across the linoleum was evidence of her longing for a break; however, there was a meal to fix, a family to feed, and my mother, regardless of her condition, never said no to us.

I crept down to the landing, listening to her talk with father, their words grating against the pleasant melody of supper preparations.

"I don't know what I'm going to do," father said.

"Did you call Frank?"

"Like I need Frank."

"You need—"

"Please, dear, don't lecture me. Not today."

My father had been out of a job for months. There were mornings when I'd thump downstairs, and he'd be in the living room, nodding off before a muted morning news show. Eating breakfast in the kitchen, I'd examine the red circles he left in the classifieds—the fine print paragraphs that mentioned experience, skills, references, and a whole host of other intimidating words. Then there were afternoons like this, when he lurked around the kitchen as my mother scrounged up supper, and inevitably, she would suggest some kind of solution—this time Frank, her stepfather, who was in charge of dorm maintenance up at the university and might just have an opening.

"Your clever little son got his bike ripped off today," fa-ther said, inevitably.

"What?"

"Get this: He goes into the store. He leaves it unchained."

"And it's gone?"

"Like the goddamn wind."

"What are we going to do?"

"Do you know how much—?"

"Yes, honey."

"Well, do you know," he said over several exaggerated thunks of knife against cutting board, "if it was up to me, he'd never get another single thing again."

"How can you say that?"

"Remember that camera I got him for Christmas? Do you remember what happened to it?"

"Please, could you keep your voice down?"

"Click, click, crack all over the sidewalk!"

"Paul."

"I should just shit my money down the toilet."

"I've had a long day. I'm tired."

A wooden spoon thudded against a stainless steel pot, and their conversation turned to mumbles.

Upstairs on my bed, I picked at an imperfection in the bedspread, teasing out a noose of thread and winding it around my index finger. I twisted until the blood surged into the fingertip, a dark balloon ready to burst. Out my window Mr. Frain was cutting his lawn. He suddenly halted, and the blast of the engine faded into the desultory sounds of the early evening. Mr. Frain stepped around the mower and extracted from the thick grass a small plastic object—an action figure, one of the many toys Jimmy frequently abandoned to the elements. He gave it a pat on the head and walked it to the back steps. Returning to the mower, Mr. Frain yanked at the cord and continued on his way towards the back fence, his skillful whistle dancing across the roar, freshening the foul smell of gasoline and grass.

***

The next morning, mom was at work, and father was away for some sudden meeting with Frank. I was to stay around the house in case the police phoned about the bike. They'd told mom not to be hopeful, but before leaving, she gently grasped my shoulder and said, "stranger things have happened"—her stock maxim for cheering me up. Lying on the living room floor, I ate cereal dry from the box and watched Daffy Duck get his neck rung, tongue shooting out like a party favor, eyes plumping like franks on the grill. That morning, I would have enjoyed seeing a cartoon in which the characters actually died. I think I would have belly laughed at that.

By noon, there was no call from the police, so I got dressed and went out back to bounce a rubber ball against the concrete steps. Father had finished these stairs earlier in the summer, in those still optimistic days when he was almost thankful to be unemployed, since it gave him time to tend to home improvement projects he'd been talking about for years. As I continued to throw, I began to see father hovering like a ghostly batter, not in his Indians cap, smoothing the concrete with a trowel, but with that scowl he shot at me from the other side of the bed, his face contorted by the loss of money he didn't really have. I threw harder and harder, the ball leaping back to sting my hand behind the glove. Father hung in there, crowding the imaginary plate, challenging me with a home run hitter's glare. Wham! Wham! Wham! I may have lost my bike, I thought, as I continued whipping the ball. But you lost your job. And how much was that worth? Huh? A whole Wham! bunch Wham! more.

Jimmy appeared at the fence, his small hands tugging on the links.

"My father doesn't want people doing that," I said, ramming the ball against the worn webbing of my mitt. "The post is coming loose." The other day, when father spied me climbing over the fence to retrieve my ball, he strode out onto those stairs of his and said in a level voice: "Go around. If I've got to tell you again, I'm going to crack you good."

"Where's your bike?" Jimmy said, continuing to jingle the fence.

"Shut up."

"What do you mean?"

"Look, I'm going to come over there and beat you up," I said, squeezing the ball, cocking my arm at him.

"Well I'll sic my dog at you."

"I'll kill you both." I couldn't quite believe what I was saying, but when I saw Jimmy's eyes bloom with fear, pleasure prickled across my skin.

"You won't," he said, but his voice was less cocksure than concerned.

I marched over to the fence. Everyday, Jimmy's mom made him lunch, cut the sandwich in fours, and placed it on a tray table with a small bag of chips and a glass of milk. Sometimes, she would invite me to come over and we'd sit on the swing together, scraping our shoes across the surface of the porch, rushing through the turkey or ham to get to the fresh baked cookies we knew were coming next.

"I saw your daddy smack you." In a sudden fit of bravery, Jimmy stuck his head over the fence like a tongue.

"Is that right?"

"You were crying."

Before Jimmy had a chance to breathe or move—before his lips had the chance to curl in mockery—I seized his hands in mine, pressing them like putty into the metal links of the fence as hard as I could, for as long as I could forget about what I was doing. The lids of my eyes fell, and on the black field before me appeared an image of my father, hand cupped and descending, striking with expert economy. When I released Jimmy's hands, he held them in front of his eyes for a moment, like the corpse of a beloved pet, then ran wailing into the house. Rust flakes on my fingertips made me think of blood.

***

The temperature climbed that afternoon, and by the evening, the humidity was murderous. Despite the box fan laboring in our kitchen window, father looked weak. He was shirtless, soft breasts sagging through a tangle of graying chest hair. Between gulps of family steak, he breathed audibly.

"I'm a grown man," father said, his mouth full of meat. "I'm not painting dorm rooms."

Mom's fork stopped half way to her mouth, two peas perfectly balanced between the tines. She slid them through the narrow opening of her lips, chewing softly, her eyes closed.

"You don't care about my pride."

"Could we talk about this later?" mom asked, eyes still closed, following the goings on of some better world of her own.

Father took a long drink of milk. I watched his Adam's apple bob.

"Any idiot could do that job is what I mean. Even your son here, if he could hold onto his brush and—"

"Shut up," mom said. The words slipped out so softly, so imperceptibly, like a noxious gas. They wafted around the room, giving density to the silence. It was the first time I'd ever heard mom say such a thing, and I half expected him to rise and crack her on the thigh. Instead, his mouth shrank. His eyebrows climbed, forming fatty scribbles of skin across his head.

Later, from the sanctuary of my room, I watched Jimmy and his father playing catch. All of Jimmy's movements were awkward. He dropped the easiest of tosses, but Mr. Frain just punched his glove and said: "Good try, good try, now toss it back. Lead with your opposite leg."

"Come down here, please," father's voice suddenly intruded. He was in the living room, at the foot of the stairs, but it felt as if he were standing directly behind me, hot breath scalding my ear. No doubt Mrs. Frain had come over to tell my parents how I'd hurt her son. Maybe there would be a doctor's bill to pay. Maybe I would just have to apologize and endure grounding for the next two weeks. Regardless, father was certain to make me suffer in that expert way of his.

When I arrived downstairs, he was standing on the other side of the kitchen table, shirtless still, a smile contorting his face. Over his left shoulder, mom looked on, her eyelids low like shades. In front of me on my placemat was a small, brightly wrapped gift.

"Open it," father said gently, shoving his hands toward the table.

I hung onto the back of my chair. My fingers squeezed the cool, smooth wood. Father closed his eyes, waiting, giving patience a try, but it wasn't long before his thick, burly brows dive-bombed toward the bridge of his nose.

"Look," he said, slapping a hand on his pants. "This is a

good deal: you let somebody take your bike and you get a present."

"Paul," mom warned. Father had shifted his weight, and now I could see my mom's eyes rising like moons over his earth-bound shoulder. It was clear she had put him up to this, making him buy this enticing apology on the table as a way of showing he wasn't such a bad guy after all.

I held my ground, not out of malice, but out of fear—fear that my opening of the present would only lead to some future loss and obligation. Father's face turned askew, almost like seven months ago, when he arrived home late from work, a tie with sailboats sinking from his neck. "Twenty two years," he said to mom, coming from the kitchen, wiping dinner from her hands with a paper towel. "Twenty two years and they let me go." He cried, then—or rather, I remember tears trapped in his eyes. If only he would have cried now as well—if only those ledger eyes would have bunched and tears the size of birdbaths would have come tumbling down his face—I think that then, I would have done just about anything for him.

Instead, he slapped the table and screamed, "open it already, you ungrateful—"

"Paul!" Mom's hand was on his shoulder. It was rare to see them touch, but this was no sign of affection. She was simply moving him aside, forcing him back against the stove with the flat of her hand, so she could take his place across from me.

"Please open it, honey. You'll like it." There was a lifting weights kind of a look in her face.

Of course I wondered what the package contained. I was ten years old, after all. The box was roughly the size of my head—the perfect dimensions for a brand new baseball glove. I imagined oiling it up in front of the jealous eyes of Jimmy Frain, pounding the tough leather of its pocket, sitting in the bleachers at an Indians game and waiting for an Andre Thornton homer.

At that moment, Jimmy's voice—girlish, taut with anxiety—sprinkled through the open kitchen window. "Over here dad!" he called. In the ensuing silence, the voice seemed to act like pressure to the back of father's head, forcing it down, his eyes off me now and onto the wrapping paper, its yellow stars flaring out against an enervated blue. I saw the florid surface of father's skull between wisps of hair.

Mom pushed him in my direction, and, after some resistance, he shuffled around the table. Palming my head, he forced it into his stomach in some awkward version of a hug. I smashed shut my eyes and squeezed with all my might, tasting hair and perspiration. The two of us formed a passable impersonation of love, yet neither mom nor father knew what I was really doing: driving father's damp flesh back into organs and bone, crushing him, killing him, making him pay, old fat man that he was.

Late for Play

Dad struck every single hole on Pearl. Mom's head beat soft time against the passenger side window. I straddled the backseat hump, the seatbelt unlocked but resting on my legs, looking through the breach between the bucket seats at the open ashtray crammed with frustrated stubs of cigarettes. We were bound for Southland Shopping Center to buy the navy blue pants and pallid Oxford shirts that St. Paul's decreed. Mom didn't like the Catholics much, having been (as she said) force-fed their fear and guilt and obscene superstition for eight long years, but she knew for certain that St. Paul's would save me from the hell of public school punches or pocketknives or worse. Dad was far from happy with this plan. More than once throughout that summer he mumbled, "Sure, you take my money. I'm good enough for *that*."

We pulled into the crowded shopping center lot. I saw a family heading out of Sears, a contented mom and dad trailing daughters who swung held hands, their round eyes darting both ways before they skittered across the lot toward their station wagon, which pointed north, toward my house, where E.J. probably had the teams split up for wiffle ball by now, and his father off the front porch swing to be official pitcher. I could almost hear the laughter, the happy thrust of fists in gloves, the high-pitched whack of plastic bat meeting plastic ball.

***

Sears stunk badly of back to school. The smell wafted from the stupidly cheerful sale signs draped across the aisles; from the stiff and uncomfortable clothes skewered by hangers and jammed onto circular racks; even from the adolescent automatons ringing up merchandise between sad sips of pop from cardboard cups. While Dad escaped to the main aisle to sift through remainder bins, Mom led me through the Boys Department until my arms were full. Then it was off to the dressing room, where I danced and shook into shirt and pants, still clinging to the idea that this could all be done quickly—that I could get back home with just enough light for an at bat or two. More than anything, I wanted to be laughing off the jeers from Jody, Boog, and E.J. as I stood at the plate; smashing a shot over everyone, as I usually did; then scampering around the bases, while Mr. Bliss did something crazy like pelt me with buckeyes and holler, "you're out, you're out, you're out, that's three!"

Hope slid from my face when I ripped the dressing room curtain aside and saw Mom's brows pinch like tweezers. "The hem is too short," she complained. "The neck is much too big. The stitching—they expect you to pay good money for this?" As she orbited around me, pulling and pinching and smoothing, I felt seconds ooze like blood drops from my watch.

Ten minutes passed. Twenty. Thirty. Dad wandered back in view just as I emerged from the dressing room for what may have been the seventh time. Mom examined me closely yet again, and then stepped back with a handclap, exclaiming: "Now I absolutely love this!"

Dad shook a can of WD-40 he held in his hand.

"What do you think?" she asked him, her voice warbling with uncertainty half way through the question.

Dad looked her up and down. Up again and down.

"Shut up," Mom said, as if he'd already spoken.

Dad just sighed and tapped a finger at his watch. There was this police drama on at nine, and he watched it faithfully despite the weekly objections of Mom, who sat down for a look three weeks ago and promptly got back up, muttering about all the sex. "You'd make a good one of them," Dad shouted into the kitchen to where she had retreated. "Maybe you should even join the nuns. You've got at least one of those vows down like a pro!"

I was coloring on the dining room floor at the time. I finished my picture in thick swirls of gray and brown and black.

***

Back in the car, the acrid smoke from Dad's newly lighted cigarette making me nauseous, I tried to calculate how many minutes it would take to get home, how many seconds it would take for me to bolt to my room and grab my glove and get back downstairs, out of the house down five doors to where the wiffle ball game was in full, luxurious swing.

Dad broke hard for slowing traffic, and we all lurched forward.

"Don't think you're doing anything when you get home," he said suddenly, as if the transcript of my thoughts had just tickered under his nose.

"But you said I could play."

"You've got a bath to take," Mom said softly. "We're dropping you off at grandma's tomorrow at nine."

Last night at the supper table, Mom explained that she and Dad had to meet with a doctor in order to discuss some things about their lives.

"Things? Like what?"

Mom put out a hand in my direction, the tips of her fingers, all those pretty crimson nails, lying across my placemat. Dad tossed a butter knife over our heads and it landed in the sink. He said, "We're going to have a nice little conversation about your mom, because she's got problems being a wife, isn't that right dear?" Mom looked straight ahead; slowly then, and surely, the air seemed to come right out her eyes.

"You said that if I had all my homework done and my room—"

"We can't always do what we want," Mom explained. "Sometimes . . . we make sacrifices . . . so that other people can do what they . . . feel they need to do."

At that moment, a series of long trucks thundered past, heading south on Pearl. On the back of each vehicle was a different carnival ride: an ornate miniature Ferris wheel, its vacant carts swinging excitedly; a merry-go-round with unicorns, horns like golden drill bits boring into the sky; and then, most stunning of all, the smooth sinuous blue of a fiberglass water slide. The trucks were coming from a festival in Parma—the one I'd pointed out the other day in the *Friday* magazine. Dad had stood over me reading, drops from his beer plunking onto the advertisement, blurring the words and pictures. "Sorry son," he said. "Your mother isn't into fun."

Monday was right around the corner. This evening might be the last chance I'd have to play ball with E.J. and the gang before the new school year began. I felt a seizure of panic. While I squirmed in my uniform and endured the admonishments of shrouded, wrinkly women, the guys would continue to meet at recess for paper football games. At lunch they'd continue to tell dirty jokes until milk came out their noses. After school, they'd head off to Brookside Park to ride the trails. By the time I took my busses home, their phone messages would be irrelevant. And when winter came—snow and cold and all that early darkness—I'd never see them again. They'd have their sleepovers and maybe call me for the first one or two, but after awhile it would be as if I had never existed. I wanted to scream; instead, in my frustration, I inadvertently kicked the back of the seat.

"That's it," Dad said. "You're taking a bath and going straight to bed. No TV or anything."

"But I didn't do—"

"You kicked the seat."

"It was an accident!"

Dad's eyes swelled in the rearview mirror.

"And you never buckled your belt. I warned you."

I turned to the back window. The carnival trucks were gone, of course, but I still saw their cargo clearly in my mind: the tremendous wheel, the otherworldly merry-go-round, the blue blue slide.

Dad ran the light at Snow. A few horns blared.

"Do you want to kill us?" Mom asked, her voice low and indifferent.

"Trust in the Lord."

"Don't start—"

"Aren't you now a bride of Christ? Don't you have some sort of 'in'?"

Mom pulled a cigarette from the pack on the dash and placed it between her lips. Dad reached across and batted it to the floor.

"When we get home," he said. "Look . . . You and me . . . after he goes to bed, we're going upstairs, dammit . . ."

Instinctively, I clicked my belt.

"I don't believe you," was all Mom said.

The words worked just like a period, quiet but definitive at the end of a long, complex sentence. The silence made me think of the previous Sunday, when Mom took me to a Catholic church service. "You'll have to go to these once a month," she said, "so you should have some idea." We sat in the back corner, safe and unobtrusive. Above was a stained glass window angled open for air. A colorful, elongated man, his eyes huge with agony, peered down at me. Then a burly priest who'd been intoning prayers and such for what seemed like hours suddenly bounced off the altar and down the aisle, swinging a silver genie lamp from side to side and creating balloons of smoke that drifted toward the pews. I put a hand over my face and tried to hold my breath against what I was sure were poison fumes.

At last, Dad bumped up over the curb in front of our house and rammed the shifter into park. We walked in a somber line toward the house—Mom first, then Dad right on top of her, each thudding up the wooden stairs. I stopped to look down the street for Mr. Bliss, the heavy bag of clothes banging at my leg. All was quiet except for the harrowing buzz of the streetlight. It was nearly dark—too late for baseball, for the carnival, for summer itself. But not too late for what happened later, after my bath and Dad's favorite cop show, when Mom closed my door behind her kiss and walked across the hall, where minutes later I heard the two of them in low voices at first, then the springy sounds of the bed and Dad's voice, Dad's strong voice only, then its gradual faltering, like he was young again, and out of breath from playing.

Brother and Sister and Love

Brother comes home from a rained out game to his fifteen year old sister pulling up panties and a glimpse of untied shoes, lace tips ticking, rubber soles thumping through the kitchen and the back door toward the dusk.

"Oh-my-God—" Sister cries, eyes crushed into her face. "You can't tell Mom!"

Later, Brother pounds his glove while watching a comedy on TV. A cream skulled man in boxers falls with a ladder from his lover's bedroom window, the boisterous laugh track following him into prickly bushes, and all Brother sees is Sister's down there hair—that shock of black before the panties rushed back into place, before she slapped on the makeshift shroud of her skirt. Tell Mom? The woman simply doesn't have the time, home for hellos between the factory and the bar, punch pressing by day and pouring dollar shots half way through the night. Her husband, the smiling anchor of her life, is now a five full years dead. Tell Mom? Why not give her a break—let her enjoy the fantasy of fine, upstanding children.

Brother cannot sleep. No, he's counting like sheep the

ways he should kick the shit out of Untied Shoes, for he's sure he knows who it is, this scrawny, tattooed dude who draws dicks on desks for fun, and tomorrow Brother could go to school and slam him against a restroom wall. He's got Father's knife, one the old man used to whittle the little boats Brother sailed as a child. He's not averse to carving a crude little warning into this scrawny dude's behind. But, in the end, what good is that going to do? Cut one up, and another will take its place. They're out there—the dudes, the untied shoes, all those prancing pricks—popping against windows like bees stupid with pollen. During some unaccounted for hour of the day, one of them is bound to work his way in for the sting.

Sister, of course she knows what Brother has been thinking, pushes into his room that night, parachute pants and the brown cocoon of a sweater like some apology for the undress of the afternoon. He sits up in bed, waiting to hear the lesson learned.

"You know I'm growing up," Sister says, hands on her hips. "And I'm gonna do what I'm gonna do."

And Brother, sighing, says: "It doesn't solve anything."

"What doesn't?"

"You think it is the answer. Like you do it, and you'll be born again or something."

"What are you talking about?"

"The, you know . . . Don't make me say it."

"For your information," she says, "I am in love."

"Well . . . in that case," Brother laughs, sliding back down under the sheets, turning toward the wall, thinking how Father, a few months from his diagnosis, used those very words, and Mother turned red as her sweater with the giant Christmas tree, and Sister cried "nooooo" before stomping hands over ears out of the laugh crazy kitchen.

The light from the hallway narrows and disappears, and Brother, in the dark again, hears Sister bound down the stairs and out the door like it's the first day of summer vacation. His heart squats in his chest, a cold, shrink wrapped chunk of furniture. "Don't come crying to me," is all he can say to the Sister who is already too far gone to hear—"Don't come crying to me" because it's not like a banged head on a table corner or a spill from your pinked out trike. No, it's more like breaking, and entering, a criminal act Brother felt only after the one time he was done, the girl spread across her comforter, dopey eyes off on some bliss filled trip of love that crash landed somewhere between the first missed period and the second. Then he broke and entered again, a crime upon a crime, this time through the women's room window of the bar where Mother works, through the window and to the back office for which he had a key, lifted from Mother's room where she slept in smoke choked clothes—to the office because he knew that's where she always brought the evening's take before sliding down her skirt for the guy who cut her checks, a nice enough man (Brother'd shook his hard hand in this office once, in fact), but, all said and done, just another bee with better shoes.

Brother swiped five hundred right from the top, twenties and tens, hard to believe, right there in his hands, sure he was going to get caught but the Mother Lover did not even have an alarm, and then, breath held out the window and all the way back home, he fell into bed for a few busted hours of sleep before school, thrusting out balls of cash toward the girl at the end of the day as she grabbed hard cornered books from a locker shelf, eyes looking past the boy that now for her had simply ceased to be. He watched as she slid the bills into her bag and turned and strolled through the buzz of students, turning milky in the glare of double doors. How young she was, this sister and this daughter and, good God, the things that he had done in the name of love, first the breakings and the enterings—the grabbing of what he could—and now this awful recompense, lounging like an undiscovered growth behind the zipped up lips of her shiny name brand purse.

TWO

Someday Morning

You're at your desk, eyes blearing over textbook prose that flows across the page with the viscosity of tenured professors. And I'm stretched across my bed, palms cradling the flat spot on my head, taking in sounds of football and wrinkled snack food bags from the common room. Sunrays flirt across my face then disappear. A toilet flushes. Next door, Greg Privett unleashes a cacophonous fart, fitting punctuation for another plotless Sunday.

What's say I swing by your dorm, take this college-ruled, 8" X 11" blank sheet of paper day, and scrawl upon it a story to remember? Not some corpse-heavy tragedy or box office blockbuster with state of the art effects. Just a short, modest narrative that begins with Giotto's, drumming our fingers at the pick up window until Dominic finally hangs up with his on-again-off-again Angela and grumbles toward us, sauce-smeared apron and all, sliding a pencil from his ear and watching with crust burning eyes while we gaze at the menu over his head, savoring all the options on our tongues, until tension has been kneaded to perfection and you order the ten, no the twelve, no the fourteen inch

Fresco Peruzzi—with extra cheese, please.

Then, as in any story worth its salt, the gut aching suspense, which we'll attempt to subdue with a stroll down Bell Street, pressing hands against storefront windows to marvel at the grain of antique bureaus and chairs—the dream furniture that will one day grace the house we vaguely plan to share. We'll cross the pedestrian bridge, swinging hands, watch the Buckeye ambling beneath us, into and out of town, like some sordid guest in the four-star hotel of our lives. All of this walking and gawking and talking in a feeble effort to keep our minds off those succulent toppings baking on the olive oiled canvas of our pie: pepperoni slices, sweating like sun bathers; red peppers, curling like smiles, portabella mushrooms plumping like love. We'll wait until we just can't take it anymore, and then, spasms of deep-dish passion flashing through our bellies, we'll clatter back over the bridge, arms out, devouring the air like hungry planes.

Alas, there will be complications—a scene that will have us chugging down Bell to Cross, curling around old men doddering down the sidewalk, slicing through handholding lovers, darting across the street, your held up hand keeping Corollas and Escorts at bay, all the while me holding the cardboard box with fingers and thumb and thinking ummm, ummm, ummm—how glorious you'll be if we can only get you there, over across the street, where we'll fling ourselves like seed onto the college green, throw open the steam-soggy cover, only to realize—no napkins!

In a burst of inspiration, I'll scroll down my plump tomato-colored sleeves and they'll do in a pinch, not that you'll be too concerned, already lifting a sagging slice to your watering mouth, plunging into a well-deserved climax of melted goo, laughing at the suspension bridge of cheese streeeeeetching from crust to oil-shiny lips, at this masterpiece of a moment—this scrumptious slice of life.

If all that weren't enough, as we sit dazed, bursting like we've just consumed a wing of the campus museum of art, scrawny Jeff Eddleman will sear by in his sun orange Nova, drumming the horn, craning out the window to say he'll catch us at Open Mike's at nine, where, in the world's longest denouement, we'll sing honky-tonk tunes we don't much like, and drink our fair share of Rolling Rock, while Jeff, wasted as a plot device, slouches in the sticky booth reading beer bottles, bending his lips and tongue around the transcendental syllables of "Latrobe."

As last call threatens, Stockton Rife, perpetual grad student, poet laureate of Clerestory, Ohio, will teeter up on stage, stroke his Walt Whitman beard to a pencil point, and for the hundred-thousandth time call our town of transients a woman, "flatchested, but warm." Drunk, tired, mourning the end of this unprecedented day, we'll feel the bell tinkle of truth in his words, experience sharp pangs of guilt over ever plotting out our futures, scheming to forget this place like some trashy summer read.

***

Years later, in the sprawling city of your birth, a competent husband snoring beside you, you'll suddenly rise and drift to the window where dawn whites the pane like a blank page from a book. On that someday morning, forearms bumping in the brown leafy breeze, you'll stand engrossed, not quite knowing what you're looking at until, through some inexplicable science of the mind, you're in the middle of our now classic text, savoring the words that stand in now for sights and smells and tastes . . . and for all the splendid arrhythmias of our early love. You'll read closely, yet revise as well, adding and deleting, scrupulously sculpting me into the man I neither was nor would grow to be, bringing back some brand new version of what may have been the greatest story of your life, or close.

I hear the doubtful strains of your voice. I see those hazel eyes marbling into your skull. Well, it's my story. It will end as I see fit.

Whack

Rachyl was gorgeous, so Greg excused in her way too many things, like munching in this cavalier manner, slouched in the chair, flecks of potato chips snowing onto her Juicy Couture.

"He's a sign," Greg said of the man she'd dubbed "Side Sack Whack," who'd passed the diner window for the third time now. Lowering his voice, eager to be ominous, Greg said, "Like a ticking bomb."

Rachyl nodded a few times, well past the limit of her attention span, then lifted blouse to mouth to vacuum the crumbs of potato chips.

"Let me do that," Greg said.

"Uh, maybe next time."

"I've got a better angle." Bashful hadn't worked for Greg these last few weeks, so he'd been trying on audacity. It didn't fit, of course—too tight in the figurative crotch—but he was not going to endure the further embarrassment of taking it back.

Rachyl pounded on the window. "Whack! Whack! Whack!" she cried, just like a duck.

On cue, Side Sack Whack—almost sporty in fleece and a cream colored baseball cap, a leather bag loose around his neck—ticked by the window again.

Greg clung to a smile just long enough to keep Rachyl thinking she was funny. Then he looked back down at the *Crux*, where the police blotter listed other Whacks who'd been doing their best to add to the gritty charm of this urban university. Three muggings, two physical assaults, a drive by shooting, an attempted rape in the last ten days—and all within the so-called "Bubble," the commercial thoroughfare between campus and town. "Travel in groups," the article advised. "Let friends know where you'll be." "Be aware." "Look like you know what you're doing."

While they were at the counter, adjusting book-clunky backpacks and waiting for some change, Rachyl said, "When he comes by again, grab his bag and see what's inside."

"Are you out of your mind?"

"It's the middle of the day. We're in The Bubble." Rachyl patted him on the cheek. "Think you'll be okay."

If audacity was too constricting, then pusillanimity fit him like a pair of Sunday morning sweats. Greg reddened, a mixture of embarrassment and anger. How many hours had he wasted in this diner today? Two? Three? Lattes, hummus plates, slices of raspberry cheesecake—how many dead presidents had he kissed goodbye over the last few weeks in an effort to open her up?

Outside, Rachyl tucked silky hair under her knit hat. She

bit her lower lip. She donned pink mittens and rubbed her straw mushroom nose. The whole point, Greg thought through gritted teeth, was to be adorable.

"Here it comes!" she sang, pushing Greg toward Side Sack Whack, who strode down the sidewalk, gathering steam, the black leather bag an ominous football at his side. The man looked winded, his mouth gulping air, his pale face glistening with sweat. He looked determined too: hell-bent, terroristic. Across the way, two security guards stood on the pedals of their bikes, heads tilted curiously, hands on hanging radios.

"Now," Rachyl said, giving him another shove.

As the strange man passed, Greg chicken pecked at the strap of the bag. That's when he saw the parted zipper teeth, the yawning void. Greg was taking a course in primitive art, and the blackness reminded him of terrible things: a cave, a world before fire, animal blood smiling against rock. He dropped his hand and watched Side Sack Whack puff down the street.

"Oh, you have no balls!" Rachyl said, blowing bangs like shrapnel into the air.

Greg reached out to touch her on the cheek, the chin, a breast. It was to be a quick, definitive portent of potency; at that moment, though, Rachyl turned, and his fingers plunked clumsily against her collarbone. The contact felt so good—so right—his fingers came back a fist. Rachyl stumbled into a garbage barrel, face wrinkling like a paper bag. The shouting of guards sounded so much like encouragement that Greg, his mouth agape, lobbed another one. This time, an explosion of tears.

The newspaper in the diner had said, "Look like you know what you're doing," and, if nothing else, Greg was trying the advice on for size.

Retroactive Special

Belinda wanted the first time to be special, but it was August, the afternoon sloppy with humidity, and they were, despite medication, sniffing and dripping from ragweed and, because of medication, languid in their lovemaking. Things got so bad at one point that Pat had to extricate himself and hop hop toward the dresser for a blow. He was gentleman enough to bring back a tissue to draw across her nose as well, a gesture that *might* have made the occasion special, all bodily fluids being equal.

But so much conspired against them! Not only their noses but their clothes—the recalcitrant zipper of his khaki shorts, her well wound scrunchie, the unnecessary (she thought) and hasty removal of which nearly cost Belinda her ponytail—not to mention the obnoxious roar of a neighbor's mower, the comically incongruous soundtrack (Journey's "Separate Ways" blaring from the dresser top TV) and, last but not least, Pat's brand new ankle cast, which thumped hideously against the bedpost like a club against a skull.

For awhile, for something to do, Belinda studied the white clumps of deodorant under this skinny boy's arms.

Then she turned to the TV and watched grown men badly handle invisible musical instruments. When Pat started chuffing like a train, she had to yank an ear to remind him there was someone else involved. Instantly, he became alert, solicitous; for awhile, he even seemed to be on to something. But soon he was flying solo again, and before she could regain his attention, he was babbling in tongues, eyeballs skittering around that shaggy haired head.

She wasn't sure if he was going or coming.

Until, that is, it was over, and he stroked her shoulder for a job well done before rising from the bed, prefacing his getaway with some barely audible thank yous and one distinctly unspecial "Guess I'll see you in trig" as he pulled up his shorts and ferreted his head back through a pinstriped polo shirt, retrieving his crutches and going, at last, with a flaccid wave of the hand that made her think about what he'd just put back in his shorts. The whole absurd episode began to dissipate with her first quiet moment alone and the next, the obligatory look in the mirror, the absentminded brush out of her hair, the long hot shower, the hours somehow filled until mushroom pizza appeared with her work-harried parents and, afterward, a glass of skim milk and a few chocolate chip cookies on the nightstand, a corpulent romance in her hands instead of homework, her back against two flat pillows on that curiously untransformed bed. Hours passed into days, days that brought the new school year to some dull approximation of life, the banal routine of English and Math and History and Gym and Lunch and Yearbook afterward—that and the countless little things that made time go, including other moments with Pat, nodding at him in a crowded hallway, exchanging vapid pleasantries before class or by banging lockers, never again seeing him in the same way as that one August afternoon, time rushing against time just past until the weeks became months and the months became prom night with other people, and graduation, both rites of passage gone in a camera flash, gone like the summer that followed sizzling on their heels; then, amazingly, another August, this at another school—a regionally prestigious university—weeks and months of surveys and seminars, of dorm room carousing and dollar drafts gulped down in sticky floored bars . . . weeks and months collecting into semesters—two, four, six, eight, and, just like that, the real world, the first big job, the years then really starting to move, filling up with locations and relocations, the making and unmaking of friends, the births of wrinkly nieces and nephews, the deaths of wrinkly grandparents—all of these things rushing against those few moments where Pat wandered between her legs, rushing, she thought more than once, like the powerful spray of that long post coital shower those many years ago, whooshing away the evidence of their—or, to be cynical, his—act, making it almost impossible for her to believe it had even happened at all.

Twenty years and it's August once again. Belinda had experienced a fit of sneezes earlier in the morning, a smidgen of sinus pressure, but such are the vicissitudes of allergies that on this beautiful Saturday afternoon, poking around in the shopping district near the college, she can see and breathe and think without impediment. Young people abound, chatting and sipping complicated coffees under umbrellaed tables and on store front stoops. She loves this atmosphere, finds it especially restorative. It certainly beats going home, where there is simply nothing to do, unless she counts the task of fixing the brass knob to the front door of her house, which, on her way out to grab the paper this morning, came off inexplicably in her hand. A golden crystal ball, the knob revealed a lonely, pensive face floating in its surface. Masochist that she is, she forced a great big smile and examined all the gruesome evidence of age that face seemed happy to show.

Belinda stops in one more place—this time Heaventy Seventies (a vintage clothes and music store)—where she flips idly through old record albums she'd been crazy about as a kid. It makes her sad that nothing costs more than two dollars or three.

"Looking for something?" a voice asks, one which immediately flips some seldom used toggle switch in her brain.

Belinda looks up to find a well dressed, middle aged man standing across from her in the Ss or the Ts. It takes her several moments to remember him, because back then he was a skinny guy with black crayon scribble for hair, a thin almost hungry pie wedge of a face, and, of course, those slapstick eyeballs. Now, the hair is gone, the face filled out, and the eyes small and attentive . . . and, she has to laugh to herself, no longer slick with allergy. He's gained a few pounds too—perhaps as many as the number of years since she'd seen him last, the evening of their high school graduation, where, finding her right before the procession, he'd looked back over his shoulder in that voluminous gown and asked if she thought he was fat. When she, laughing, told him "yes," he turned around, put hands upon hips, and said with affected desperation, "But black's supposed to be so slimming!"

Pat points to a sign over her head which reads: "Special: Buy Back Your Past" and in a pitch perfect, used car salesman kind of voice exclaims: "Take an additional 30 percent off everything in the store!"

"Really?" she says, laughing, surprised at how easily she's able and ready to play along, selecting an album from the bin and playfully placing it—something by those handsome, hairy, high voiced brothers Gibb—against her chest. "Has there ever been a better deal on junk?"

Pat smiles and cruises a hand over the place where all that hair used to be. Then, abruptly, eschewing all transition, he says:

1) "It's been a long time."

2) "You look great."

3) "Let's go for a drink."

The word "no" is a brown balloon inside Belinda's stomach. She can see it squeezing up the windpipe, feel it bopping against the roof of her mouth. As it bangs against clenched teeth, however, the balloon punctures, quickly loses air, and a high-pitched yessing sound begins escaping through her lips. For a moment, she's aghast. And then she pictures the alternative: returning home at four forty-five, a single bag of groceries dangling from her hand; the obscene quiet of her house just after entering, as if sofa and TV and framed pictures and paged-through magazines are standing at attention, awaiting her hard-to-win approval; the baking of a chicken breast, the boiling of frozen broccoli; the dishes; that stupid door knob, jamming it back into the hole, trying for another hour to get it to line up with the mechanism inside the door; and maybe, if she is lucky, a half way decent rerun on cableless TV.

The more Belinda thinks about it, the more she realizes that there is no good reason to fight this yes. After all, she is in the middle of a slippery skid toward thirty eight and, clearly, as she told Anne, her one good friend, over potent drinks the night before, "The Soulmate Project" is an abject failure.

"You mean 'The *Pri*mate Project?' Anne had said, smirking into her Cosmo.

Belinda had made a face, but she recognized the truth behind the joke. Twenty years of dating these man-shaped mammals—of brain-picking friends and family for viable candidates, of scrolling through Internet profiles, of talking haltingly for that first time on the phone, of settling on a place for the disturbing public spectacle of their date, and then, of heading out, still fretting over makeup and attire, struggling to find common ground over white clothed tables, having these men look at her as if she were a car in a showroom (which, to be fair, was—give or take a metaphor—the way she sometimes looked at them), excusing herself to restrooms for soul searching that masqueraded as primping in the mirror, and, on more than one occasion, coming *this* close to climbing out an especially inviting window and making a mad dash for home; of movies and museums and nature hikes, the long, dreadful process of getting to know someone, being both excited and depressed—excited because, after all, who knows, he could be *the one*, depressed because if he wasn't then why was she even wasting the time? All of this energy—physical, intellectual, emotional, other types of energy for which she as yet had no name—and what does Belinda have to show? Vague memories of a couple dozen well prepared meals, a few good conversations about literature or politics; a piece of jewelry or two, a second experience of sex and a third—each of which, despite their moments, a far far far orgasmic cry from special.

But now, this relatively handsome man—this Pat, or at least the few pleasant vestiges of the Pat she still remembers—is asking her out, and since she already knows him that's one prodigious anxiety out of the way, which, when she thinks about it, makes her feel much better about the whispered yes that has since turned into a definitive "sure!," strolling now with him towards the register, one hand clutching the face of three old grade school heart-throbs, the other brushing against stretch shirts and denim minis and stirrup pants. She pauses by a rack of stonewashed jeans. The one pair she still might be able to squeeze into looks so pale and threadbare that she fears it could very well fall apart right in her hands.

"I'm getting all my favorite CDs on vinyl," Pat explains at the register, tapping the stack he has collected.

"Aren't you supposed to do it the other way around?"

"*Do it*," Pat says, eyebrows dancing.

She wants to whack him with her Bee Gees.

"*The other way around.*"

She laughs—a gulp, a snort, silly like a sixteen year old. If he's going on eight, the least she can do is meet him halfway.

Twenty minutes later, in the smooth dark no time or place of a nearby upscale pub, they've laughed themselves well back into the past, slipping through even that door behind which their first meeting gathers so much dust. Remember, he says, it was in the principal's office, where she was filing paperwork to help pay for her tuition and he shuffled into the office behind Chuckhole Chudinski, their officious and acne scarred principal, who demanded to know where the disposable razors were, as if she would know.

"You think you are a man, Mr. O'Connell," Chudinski had said, rifling through his desk drawers while Pat made expert monkey faces at Belinda. She had to smack a manila folder against her face to keep from laughing out loud.

Suddenly, Chudinski said, "ah ha!" and plucked a razor from his coffee mug pencil holder. He put the blade up to the fluorescent light to see if it would do a good enough job before tapping it on the tip of Pat's nose and, invoking the irrefutable power of private school policy, ordering him to shave.

"Where?" Pat asked.

"The bathroom."

"I mean, what part of my body?"

"Don't be smart, Mr. O'Connell. It does not become you."

"Do I get extra credit if I shave all this?" Pat asked, pulling up his wrinkly white Oxford so the principal could see the dark hair coiling around his nipples.

Belinda sips her drink and smiles, even though she shouldn't because, after all, that was the moment that led to what she thought had been long ago rubbed out of her mind.

"For Chuckhole," Pat concludes, "foliation was worse than fornication."

She laughs, and then, just like that, one of those unpredictable awkward silences ensues. At a loss for something to say, each becomes seriously preoccupied with the antics of other patrons, the long at bat in the third inning of a baseball game on TV, the black and white memorabilia posted on the wall nearby. Belinda takes a long first sip of her second drink and begins to feel disoriented. Is she really here with this man who used to be the boy who lunged on top of her? Is she really a woman now, in her late thirties, single and alone? How do such things happen, and who is responsible?

"You know," Pat says at last, drinking deeply from his beer. "Back then, that time, that one time . . ."

It's coming back, spurred on by the alcohol perhaps, re-appearing at any rate against her will. The dim outlines. The colors. The sounds. A sharp image of her feet in the air, framing a poster (of Rick Springfield, was it??), flits across her brain.

I have to tell you . . . I was bad."

"Gee, you think so?" Vertiginous from the vodka, Belinda clutches the table to maintain balance. She realizes she's starved, not having eaten since that crumbly cereal bar on the trip into town.

"Yeah, I was bad. Then, afterward, I felt bad. Then I just, you know, wanted to get out of there."

"I wanted it to be special."

"Special?" Pat says, clapping his hands together. "Who's to say it won't be?"

What a line! Belinda thinks a few or several moments later, on her unintentionally circuitous way to the bath-room. What does it mean? she thinks on her weavy way back, the answer seeming to come when she notices Pat settling with the bartender and laying down a handsome tip, as if, now that the reacquaintment (she's not thinking clearly; is that even a word?) is out of the way, it's on to Phase Two, which, she guesses correctly, involves going back to his place. She should be angry; she should throw someone's beer in his face, place a pump in his presumptuous crotch. Instead, another yes just hisses through her lips, and, the next thing she knows or cares to notice, she's in the passenger seat of his convertible, a beautiful car, she says, knowing nothing about cars herself, a realization that makes her want to laugh. The two screwdrivers have seemingly dismantled her brain, so she simply closes her eyes and allows the wind to push hair and thoughts and everything right out of the way.

Pat was not a dedicated student in high school, yet his apartment has a distinctly academic feel to it. In place of where she might have put her 25 inch TV is a telescope on a tripod, its thin white neck craning toward the sliding glass door to the balcony. On three walls there are books—ratty paperback classics, awkwardly sized hardcovers about art and architecture, reference guides for language and music and outer space.

"Look around," he says, "I'm going to change and find us something to eat."

He disappears down a hallway while Belinda drifts around the living room, looking for pictures, for cards, for certificates—for some evidence, in other words, of the life he's been leading for the half a life he has been absent from hers. Finding nothing beyond an old wedding photograph of his mom and dad (so young, so beautifully black and white!) she turns to the shelves, selecting at random a book so big she must sit down to examine it. She pages through, killing time, distracted by the sounds of cupboard doors and dishes in the unseen kitchen. Her attention is arrested at last by a full page picture of an ancient mask—a cracked wooden face with a dark, ill-formed nose and eyes that seem like holes straight back to the dawn of time. Who might have worn such a thing? And why?

"Oh, by the way," Pat says, his voice suddenly approaching. "I've just got to show you something."

"Seen it already," she says.

"No. Seriously."

She looks up, expecting (and, by this point, desperately needing) a plate of cheese and crackers or, given Pat's relentless sense of humor, a cereal bowl of microwaved pizza rolls; instead, she sees him in the doorway to the living room, in khakis and a t-shirt now, cradling some strange object—a crude husk of something, hard and white like a bone one might find on the dig she has just been reading about. The object appears to be covered by a series of colorful squiggles, which trigger something in Belinda's brain. Putting the book down on the coffee table, she walks over to him and can't help but burst out laughing because, sure enough, just as she thought, Pat's holding his ankle cast from twenty years ago. And there, directly under the foot, prominent in purple, endures her garish signature.

Belinda snaps back in time and place, sashaying into her bedroom once again, buttocks tingling behind her skirt. Just a few steps behind is the sound of Pat's impatient crutching, which thrills her beyond belief. She'd been kissed before—twice, but who was counting?; however, this moment was without precedent, a moment of pure pleasure—the giddy sense of anticipation that came with the knowledge that she had something he wanted and could determine the pace at which he acquired it. That lovely walk up the stairs and into the room—not the rushed and clunky sex that followed—had been the one truly special moment of her life. Mistakenly—and egregiously so—she had thought it was the act itself that would lift her to a higher level, out of the awkward world of adolescence into the rarified air of adulthood. She was young. She was dumb. She didn't know that life's extraordinary moments occur in the moments just before you expect them to, that they are forgotten when the so-called "special times" slap you so cruelly in the face.

Belinda draws a finger along the cast, hard and dusty like the fossil it is. She traces her magic markered name, embarrassed by her large and flamboyant script.

"Pleisto*teen* era," Pat says.

For the first time since she's known him there's no funny face. In fact, the lips twitch and the now glassy eyes make it look as if he might just cry. Or maybe it's just the allergies, kicking in for the night.

Belinda likes to think that Pat still wears the cast, placing it back on at night for old time's sake, just as she used to do with her dental retainer, the container for which (she suddenly recalls) she used to use as luggage for a doll she was getting too old to carry around. It thrilled her to remember that her father made a special strap for the container from a strip from one of his old belts. When the family went to the store or on a trip, Belinda made sure that the doll (Had she really named it Miss Fundella?) took the case along, made sure too that it was filled full of odd little things—a clip on earring, a penny or a nickel, a balled up list of misspelled things to do. Then, it was just something she did—the mundane idiosyncrasy of a typical suburban child. Now, however, the memory shines out at her like a tangible treasure, something to slip onto a wrist or finger.

Pat leaves her with the cast, just drops it into her hands, as if there is far more to examine—intricacies of design, unprecedented textures, secret compartments.

"I'm boiling up some pasta," he says, calling back from the hallway.

She hears the clatter of hard noodles pouring out of a box and remembers she is hungry, but at that moment it is not her stomach that growls but her brain, alive now, alert, ravenous for other lost moments that begin to return, one after the other, like doddering aunts at an extended family reunion. And there she is, the middle aged Belinda, hair tied back, face crouching behind makeup but legs still looking good in a dress the color of the sun, opening a door—a knobless door!—with an uncommon power which, after all these years, she's just now learning to wield.

Air

Ryan stood in the street behind the turned down gate of a pickup. Some troglodyte with equally gnarled hair was up in the bed, pushing a massive slab of dark stained wood toward my brother, who tried grasping it first one way and then another, before dropping hands to his side.

"Hey man," Ryan said, squinting toward the porch, placing a gloved hand over his brow. "How bout a little help?"

The central air died against a wavering wall of midsummer humidity. How could anything human be outside on such a day?

"What is that, and why are you bringing it here?" I said, placing my arms akimbo.

"Air hockey, man. We were out there yard sale-ing. Down on Sycamore they've got this huge block thing going." He slapped the table, trying to impress me (I surmised) with the sturdy craftsmanship. "Thirty-five bucks. Can you effing believe it?"

I closed the door and returned to my well-chilled living room. There was an article to finish—a fall foliage piece for *Ohio* magazine. Notes and sources lay scattered on the hardwood floor in some pretense of design.

Just as I fell back on the couch, the clumsy melody of my brother's knock sounded on the door.

"Go away," I said.

Again the knock—more awkward trills and fripperies.

I took a deep breath before thumping back to the door.

"Come on, Ben. Be a brother, and let us in." Ryan was soaked through with sweat and nearly out of breath.

I just glared—tried to scorch him like the infuriated sun; when that failed against the power of his large warped smile, I retreated to the kitchen. For Ryan, this was tantamount to an invitation. In a few moments, he and his slack-jawed companion were bumping the table in through the door. I picked desiccated fruit from a bowl of cereal while brooding over the extended ellipses of our relationship—the four full years since I'd seen him last, the eighteen-month breach before that. If I had the courage, who knows?—maybe I could have forced a happy ending: I could have lost my temper and let loose with all the things I longed to say, and Ryan would have slunk away, hand in hand with his bedraggled buddy, back under the damp and fungous rock they'd scuttled out from.

Instead, I sheepishly returned to the living room, intent on nothing more than gathering up my things and escaping to my study. The hockey table was standing now on thin, uncertain legs. The two of them had moved my coffee table out of the way and spilled a stack of guidebooks and state forest brochures. I scooped up the bits and pieces of my recalcitrant essay from the couch and pressed them against my chest. For a moment, Ryan was at a loss, his face darkened by a vague cloud of guilt. Then he thrust out a hand.

I was close enough now to breathe his wretched stink—the uncountable days of grime and sweat, compounded by the smell of these recent exertions. Additionally, there was a pungent fast food odor—some combination of raw onions and ketchup that made my stomach turn. Still, I conjured up civility, placed my things back on the couch, and grasped his glove, which (as I belatedly observed) was blackened with I had no idea.

"This is Pill," Ryan said, turning to his friend.

"Hello Bill," I said.

"It's Pill," Ryan said, nudging this creature as if he could not believe I'd made so egregious an error. "As in 'Take a pill.'"

I had learned over the years that much of the pleasure of having a prodigal sibling comes from being audacious with your disdain, so I responded with nothing more than a silent angry stare. After what I judged to be a long and uncomfortable time, I said, "I suppose you'll be wanting something . . . to drink."

"That would be kind of you," Ryan said, responding with an awkward kind of bow.

While rummaging in the refrigerator, I was struck by a sudden fear. Four years, I thought. A baccalaureate degree worth of days he'd been gone. This was certainly more than long enough to render one a *total* stranger regardless of the depth of the previous attachment. Ryan definitely looked different. Unwashed hair now straggled down to the middle of his back. A huge belly strained against a paper thin t-shirt. Then there were those eyes, which had always been intense, but now, due to the effect of whatever it was that was no doubt coursing through his veins, looked as if two powerful thumbs had wiggled behind those sockets had punched them out. What was to say that my brother was not different inside as well, capable of things more serious than I read about in the blotter pages of the *Crux*? And here I had let him in . . . and left him alone with his barbaric accomplice in the front room of my brand new home!

I rushed back to find Ryan and Pill standing idly around the humming table, hands in pockets, wearing nearly identical looks of appreciation. I gave each a bottle of spring water and told myself to relax.

Ryan cracked off the cap and took a long drink. "Nice and cool in here," he said.

Pill had folded his hands around his bottle. Perhaps he was saving it to wash.

"Come on, now. Play." Ryan held out the puck like a hand to be shaken.

The hum of the game conjured up a particularly acute nostalgia. For a few moments, it smoothed over those pot-holed years with a kind of flourish, like a knife over pure white frosting. Everything seemed temporarily fine—fine enough to take the plastic disk and set it down, fine enough to watch it drift magically across the table's tiny pores and think about those Christmases of our early adolescence, when the game was wildly popular with our friends, when our parents failed to come through for us, and we—as we did for so many things so many times—simply gave up asking. But whenever we bussed to the mall, he dragged me to one of the arcades, and we bashed that puck back and forth until our knuckles bled and our quarters were gone. On more than one occasion, the disk would leap off the table and roll away while one or the other of us went chasing it, holding our sides from laughter. Ryan would win one game and I'd win the next. It was this perfect rivalry, as much as the game itself, that kept us together through the winters of our thirteenth and fourteenth years. Once, we were in the throes of an especially vicious game, the score tied interminably at nine. Ryan, his face red with both laughter and the scalding rage for victory, blasted a shot I somehow batted away; unfortunately, the puck leapt from the surface of the table and caromed off the forehead of a security guard. Two minutes later, we were in the parking lot of the mall, prohibited from returning.

"That's a first," Ryan said, bent over with laughter. "That's a mother effing first!" We reviewed the game as we walked to the gas station across the street. With leftover quarters, I bought a can of cola, and he bought a pack of cigarettes.

Standing in the bus shelter minutes later—stamping my feet to keep the cold at bay—I looked across the street at Ryan, who was heading the other way, going to see some friends for "a little of the funny stuff." He made faces and waved stupidly for awhile . . . my twin brother, doing a horrible impression of a mirror. Then his bus pulled between us, belched a cloud of black exhaust, and he was gone.

The biased air slowly coaxed the puck toward my goal. "Come on, brother," he said. There was the old challenge in his voice again. It rose up from the depths of all those protracted absences—rose up tentatively like a head from a foxhole and I smacked at the puck as hard as I could, aiming between the eyes of that figurative head. Ryan had been standing casually, wiping sweat from his brow with the back of a hand, but he was ready, blocking the disk with surprising ease. In an instant, he was all concentration, trapping my next shot against the side of the table before setting the puck in motion again, back and forth and back and forth in front of him, like a hypnotist's watch. Then he fired. My move to block it came a full second after I heard the plastic clink of puck in goal.

"SCORE!" Ryan sang and danced in a circle.

Pill put down his water for a perfunctory clap.

I dropped the puck and fired away, but that shot—as well as all my subsequent ones—went awry. Ryan, of course, had much better luck: After every goal, he cried out, "SCORE!"—each time more vehement than the last. When the score was six to nothing, I sat down on the couch, hands against my chest as if I were feeling for bruises.

"Don't give up, man," Ryan said.

I looked up at his expectant face, those punched out eyes, the green of which reminded me of some moss I had been reading about. The article stated that there are 1800 types in America alone, but, to be honest, they all looked pretty much the same to me.

"Take it out of here," I said.

"This is a gift. I want you to have it."

"I've got no room."

"Right here, man. It fits."

"I don't want it. I didn't ask for it. Understand?"

"Why are you being so rude?" I might have expected the question from my brother, but it was Pill who spoke. There was genuine curiosity in this interloper's tone, but something else too—an undercurrent of menace. I watched a rivulet of sweat wind its way down his narrow face, toward a scar that smiled across his cheekbone. He wore a black, threadbare t-shirt and jeans with a trail of holes running up his thighs.

"This is my house."

"Well, that doesn't make it right."

"It's okay, Pill." Ryan bent down and unplugged the machine. "Let's just take her down."

Pill moved to help only after he had stared my eyes to the floor. I picked up a photocopied article detailing the best ways to protect against Lyme disease and the West Nile virus. It made you wonder why people bothered—why they were so enamored of the natural world, why they went outside at all.

Out of the corner of my eye, I saw the table fall to its side. Ryan removed the legs. Pill picked up the screws and counted them before carefully sliding them into his jeans pocket.

"The thing is," Ryan said, wiping hands against his belly. "I've tried. I've only always tried."

I flapped the notes for my article as loudly as I could.

"Trying is like my life philosophy."

Then they were sliding it out the door, Ryan in front, lifting it up at the threshold.

"That should count for something," he said as he disappeared out the door.

As soon as the table was all the way out on the porch, Pill put down his end, straightened his back with a grimace, and turned back to me.

"I ought to kick your ass," he said. I could tell he'd said the words without thinking, but his eyes, zeroing in on my surprise, seemed to warm to the idea, as if he were generating some ideal vision of the moment in his head.

Against my will, I shrunk into the living room.

"I'm not saying I'm going to do it. I was a guest in your house. But still. This is no way to treat a brother. I don't care what you think he's done. This is no way to treat him. Am I getting through to you?"

"Easy Pill, everything's cool." Ryan's voice called from

the porch. "I can sell this thing." I heard a forced laugh. "I can even make some effing money on it."

Pill shrugged and picked up his end of the game and disappeared out the door.

From the front window of my sealed up house, I watched as if Ryan and Pill were actors in a silent film, pantomiming the table back into the truck, where they dropped it down a little harder than they wanted. Ryan spent several seconds closely examining a corner. Satisfied, he gave a nod and they tied the table down before hopping in unison out of the bed. Pill gave Ryan a gentle clap on the back, and the two of them climbed in the pickup. As they eased away from the curb and down the street, the sun flashed off the passenger side window to blind me for a moment. But only for a moment. Although his powerful odor still lingered in the living room, I pushed all thoughts of Ryan aside. I willed myself into possession of my senses and plunged back into words; to my delight, I found them waiting to align in one well-researched sentence after the other, paragraph upon paragraph on all those rugged trails, those tall and vivid trees. When I finished, I loaded the printer with the highest quality paper—bright and cold and sharp as ice.

Ladies

"This gorgeous guy is sitting right there," Jilly says, pointing to the empty stool. "He's showing this just gorgeous profile: a wavy mane of what do they call it?—chestnut hair; a prominent but, you know, not bulbous nose; lean cheek sprinkled with stubble. I'm smiling, I'm staring. You know me, I'm drooling—what can I say?"

Sandra nods, dipping a pierced olive into her martini over and over again, like she's cooling it off. Beth taps a red cloth napkin at the corners of her lips and returns it to her lap.

"After awhile, he turns ever so slightly, and this white-toothed grin leaps out of that swarthy face. Did I tell you he was swarthy?"

"He's getting better all the time," Sandra says.

"So the book I'm reading falls right out of my hands and lands in this cozy little tent on the floor directly beneath him. He leans over, picks it up. 'Ah,' he says knowingly, '*Tender is the Night*,' in this voice as smooth and sweet and rich as the raspberry cheesecake I'd just devoured."

Beth says, "Did you just swoon? Man like that I would have swooned."

I nearly died of shock."

"That good?" Sandra asks, her teeth pulling the olive from its plastic sword.

"Well," Jilly begins, pupils suddenly losing luster. "Here's the thing." She stops to search her purse, removes a tin of mints, plops three in her mouth. "The thing is, he turns to face me . . . you know—to *gaze into my eyes*, and there's this—my God—this huge protuberance on the other side of his nose—"

"A growth? A goiter or something?" Beth presses her back against the stool.

"A whitehead. Absolutely h-u-g-e HUGE." Jilly throws out her arm and sings:"'Rising like Olympus above the Ser-en-get-iii . . .'"

Sandra nearly spits out her martini. "Imagine: A zit on a fully grown man!"

Slouching, Beth asks, "So what did you do?"

"Well, what else was there to do but thank him for the book, get up, and . . . bolt out the door."

"Let me get this straight," Sandra says. "You ditched this guy, this prospective 'man of your dreams,' because he had a simple pimple on his face?"

A tic of the eye serves for "yes."

"They disappear, you know."

"I know, I know." Jilly is suddenly crying. She dabs at her eyes with a cloth napkin and licks salt from the rim of her finished margarita. "But I'm thirty-six. Thirty-six!"

"Two days . . .three at the outside, and they're gone."

But Jilly doesn't hear. She's already high heeling toward the bathroom, past all the beaming brew pub youths, brash-breasted girls in booths sheltered by the strong soft arms of their blemishless boys.

Sandra holds a mint of her own to her lips. "To the innumerable benefits of the married state." She slips the small disk into her mouth and immediately makes a face, as if this weren't the texture or taste she had expected.

Beth looks at Jilly's plate of food—the flaccid bed of lettuce, the homely bun still damp from hamburger blood. She strangles the napkin on her lap.

The waiter strolls by. He's got a pen cocked behind his ear, lush black hair glistening atop an impeccable Mediterranean face. Sandra bats her eyes, runs a long middle finger around the rim of her drink.

"Ladies," he announces, like a game show host. "What else can I get you this evening?"

Sandra rests the tip of her tongue between her teeth.

"Don't give me 'ladies,' Beth says, innocuous eyes suddenly punching out of their sockets. "Do we look like fricking 'ladies,' you stupid . . . you beautiful . . . punk?"

THREE

Third Anniversary

She came back, plodding clumsily in the sand, flip flops in one hand, ice cream bars in the other.

"Thought you were going to the bathroom."

"I did."

"What's with the ice cream?"

She plopped down on the towel, kicking sand into my face.

"Beach food, silly."

"We have ice cream at home. Chocolate Marshmallow. Rocky Road."

"So?"

"We've been eating it for days."

"You mean 'you've.' *I've.*"

We ate the frozen bars in silence. They're small, and you can finish them in a minute. But there she was, long after I was done, still going at it, the white stuff oozing down all over her hand, which she had to lick because she hadn't even thought of napkins.

Execution Style

After these nine, ten, or eleven months or more, wouldn't it be great—wouldn't it just be the biggest kick—if Sal shuffled out of that CVS and all the way across the sleepless night of asphalt only to find her brand spanking dead? She's not talking plain old heart attackish dead but dead with a gruesome flourish, like that mafia guy in Bella Vista a few weeks back: slumped over the steering column, cheek melting against the wheel, eyes wide and vacant, bullet in the base of the skull.

Would serve Sal right for just about everything—like Friday, that travesty of a romantic dinner at the BYOB off South and Second. He'd insisted on beer. She wanted wine, even though she really didn't like it. They bickered in whispers at a WAWA ATM machine. The result: He drank his Miller, she her lukewarm Chardonnay. When the entrees arrived, Sal ate quickly, galloping through the Chicken Puttanesca with fork and knife. Despite the air conditioning, sweat stippled his hairless skull, like so many child sized tears on the run.

Oh, if only she could be dead yet somehow see him

come, huffing toward the car under the irate sun, sweat like black blood through his Champion tee. There'd be any number of reasons for the livid twitch of nostrils, the ominous arch of one thick brow. Maybe she'd forgotten to give him enough money for the bill. Maybe he had to swipe his maxed out credit card. Maybe he walked up and down that aisle for an embarrassing eternity, but they didn't have the ones she wanted. Seeing her prone against the wheel, he'd be sure at first to say something smart like, "Christ, now what?" figuring she'd spilled some coffee, or lost an earring, or maybe this time something really dumb—a blouse sleeve caught in the gearshift.

Her death would be perfect revenge for yesterday—the final straw—when Sal returned to his hard-assed world again, jumping into Dave's Hummer to rumble all the way down to Dover for some crazy motorcycle thing. Later—it must have been two or three am—she'd heard him clumsy on the stairs, but only to go to the bathroom.

As the sizzle of piss diminished, she called out tentatively, "Sal, please come here."

"No."

She looked at the bedroom door, felt him behind it, swaying from who knows how many 7 & 7s.

"But I need you."

"Sure you do," he said, his voice cold and flat as a speculum. "Please check the calendar for date and time."

After a moment, there were heavy shoes on the stairs,

down into the living room. The couch squeaked a few moments later as he sought a comfortable position for the night.

He'd approach the car, take in the shattered pebbles of glass, the odd wrench of her head, the frozen eyes she doubts he even knows the color of. She'd see the admonitions shrivel on his tongue, hear the first faint calls of her name as he came to understand that this flabby and familiar woman he'd sat next to and slept next to and ate next to while watching TV—his wife of eight years, his girlfriend of four before that, was D-E-A-D dead.

To see the look on his face! The way that big jaw moves back and forth when he can't balance the checkbook. The fingers in his eyes when he's about ready to lose his cool. She'd be smiling. Wherever and whatever she'd be, there'd be this great big C-section of a smile slashed across her face.

It would be perfect—absolutely perfect! . . . that is, until the *something* that would be sure to spoil it all. Not just the monthly penance hanging in the drugstore bag at his side, but something unpredictable, like a dampening of his eyes or full-fledged tears or that and more: something to hate him for and love him for, like opening that plastic bag, unwrapping and unfolding what has only taunted him from the bathroom basket months on end, using one then two to wipe the blood still trickling down her neck and pooling between her legs. This soft and reverent surprise, smooth cooing motions until she's somehow cleaned right back to life, and they have gone back home, are giggling now in bed, feasting on

carry-out and poring over so many names from a book his
pleased at last parents have sent along with love.

Left Only

Dawn would be early for the shower, but it was better than staying here, where Rick was driving her nuts with his Toby Keith and surround-sound NASCAR, his poker chips and fat cigars. It was his night to "get ugly" as he said—his once-a-month vacation from himself, a sordid trip accompanied by Joe, Damon, and whoever else happened to appear throughout the night with six packs of High Life, jumbo bags of cheese puffs, Ziplocs of weed.

Rick was her first decent boyfriend. Eleven months and (as she told her dubious mother) going strong. How dare she complain? With a minimum of grumbling, Rick would make himself scarce tomorrow, when Julie, her friend from way back, arrived with a warm hug and cream filled Glazers from QuikPik to watch movies—romantic comedies he would probably finger before leaving, searching the back of boxes for "hot chicks or nudity."

Dawn promised she'd call when she got to the shower and call when she left. In the back seat of the Aspire, she carefully arranged the bottle of wine, the spinach dip, and, of course, the gift—a sexy, scarlet and white lace chemise. She could easily see herself slipping into the cool, silky garment and striking a seductive pose on the bed or sofa. But Rick wasn't interested in such things; for him, lingerie was superfluous. It just got in the way of the stuff that mattered.

As she eased out of the drive, Dawn released an audible sigh. It was nice to have a world—even if it was nothing more than the compact bubble of the car's interior—to herself, a quiet, peaceful world if she chose, or one gently filled by the sentimental croonings on WCLR. If she had her way, she'd grab a cup of drive thru coffee and just drive—cruise Route 28 through the forest, sway to the gentle undulations of the sinuous road, tap the wheel to Billy Joel ballads, and end up where she may, heedless of time or obligation.

But she'd been invited to this shower by her boss, who last week placed a well-manicured hand on her nailbitten one and said, "You *must* come," and that meant she had to go, despite the fact that Dawn had so little in common with the women at New Start. After "How are you?" and "I'll have red," she would be speechless as usual, in silent awe of these women who had homes, sprawling places bordering the river; kids old enough for dance lessons and soccer practice; Land Rovers and Pathfinders cluttered with coolers, muddied cleats, brand name changes of clothes; physically fit, salt and peppered husbands who worked as attorneys, oncologists and plastic surgeons. Dawn did her best with thrift store skirts and blouses, but, in the context of the center, she looked like someone out of step with the times.

Not that the women cared, as long as she answered phones, made copies, kept the coffee fresh twenty-five hours a week.

Dawn found herself at a red light in the Left Only lane. In a convertible to her right, a middle-aged man, skin wrinkly as balled up aluminum foil, grinned at her. Dawn had planned to kill time driving through campus, but she could not imagine following this man, and giving him even the remotest possibility of an idea. When the light flipped to green, she puttered left instead, down Treatment Road, past the box factory, where her father had worked for years. Every Saturday afternoon, she'd be dragged by her mother across the city, where they'd wait in the tar-smelling lot for him to emerge from his inevitable overtime and fall into the passenger seat. They'd drive home to nothing more than the rhythmic thumps of tires over patched asphalt. From the backseat, Dawn would study her father's profile, hard and gray and damp as basement walls.

Out past the mall she went, past the air-conditioned world that welcomed her for a few pleasant hours earlier today, where in the delightful process of buying Sandra's gift, she'd completely lost track of time. Dawn had fallen for the garment right away, and, encouraged by the ebullience of the saleswoman (who had one her "hubby" just loved), made the purchase. On the way home, Dawn realized she'd bought it more for herself than for the lucky wife to be. But so what? That was simply the definitive sign of a gift well-chosen.

Stopped under a highway bridge, she listened to cars

rumble north and south on I 71—toward Cleveland and Columbus. She had a friend in each city, each of whom moved away to college and discovered the world—or Ohio, at least—was bigger, filled with more opportunity and wonder than the tiny town where she lived. "I was homesick at first," Kate told her on the phone some years ago now, "but then I met friends, and slowly . . . surely . . . I built this whole new wonderful life." She'd seen Tamara's name in the Class Notes of her high school publication. Dawn's best friend from grade school was a vice president of something. A vice *president*. The title struck her dumb with its power.

When the light turned, Dawn suddenly found herself out of town. The white sign on the side of the road said 45 MPH. That number—the clear, black fact of it—she found it vaguely thrilling. Stepping on the gas, leaning out the window to push her face against the rush of late summer wind, she sped into the newly paved road. It was 8:25. She'd drive a little farther—up to the next intersection (wherever that might be)—and turn around. Even if she hit a light or two on her return, she'd only be fashionably late. By then, enough of a crowd would have gathered so that Dawn could grab a paper plate of carrot sticks and dip and slide inconspicuously into the festivities.

The Aspire groaned up an unexpected hill. Not long after a sign for a dangerous curve, the pungent smell of oil reached her through the vents. According to Rick, the car had been doing this for days. "You just have to watch it," he said last week, shrugging his shoulders, on his way back to the bedroom where his video game was paused. Okay, so she would watch it. She looked down at the dash, into the dark, mysterious vents. As the smell intensified, she even stuck a finger inside, as if that would keep the odor at bay—under the hood, where all of that stuff belonged.

When thin question marks of smoke curled out under the hood, Dawn eased off the road and turned off the car. She'd let it rest. The hill was simply too much to conquer all at once. She counted to fifty, adding ten more for luck. By then, the smell had diminished, the smoke dissipated. She took that as a sign the car was getting better. Holding her breath, sliding teeth together, she carefully twisted the key. The car would not turn over. She tried it again, squeezing the key, pushing it deep into the ignition, listening as the undulating groans of the engine flattened into a dull pathetic purr. A tear of perspiration glided between her breasts. She tried it one more time (wasn't the third time a charm?)—there was nothing but a soft, ominous click.

When she was twelve years old, she'd been forgotten by her father at a skating rink. Skates slung over her shoulder, brain still buzzing with the pleasant thoughts of cute boys swiping her pink knit cap from her head, she looked left and right for the familiar bow of her father's Continental. The dusk had collapsed into dark, the traffic tapered off, and a few questionable silhouettes slunk by, the whites of eyes sneaking over dark turned up collars. Still, no sign of him. Finally—an hour late—her father had pulled up, beer on his breath but not enough to dull the serrated edge that was always in his voice. "Are you a baby?" he'd said. "A little baby that has to call mom if dad isn't right out in front like a bus?" Slumped in the seat of her disabled Aspire, she felt it all again: the adolescent shame of dependency, the scalding memory of her dead father's eyes.

After a time, Dawn climbed out of the car and stood amid the acrid fumes, hands on hips, the night encroaching, the wind confusing her hair, gnats dancing in her face. Tears shook in her eyes. During the day, this was a well-traveled road. Now, however, it seemed that most people had arrived to where they were going. And those that hadn't—those stranded souls like her—were vulnerable, subject to danger. Just last week, this young woman down in Independence had been raped. The guy had eased up to her stalled vehicle in a sleek Jaguar, stepped out dressed to the nines. Later, he'd taken her into the woods. Dawn imagined the woman's skirt dragging in the grass and mud, the sound of crickets, the suffocating press of the rapist's inhuman flesh. "It's not sex men want," her mother told her once, after Dawn had returned home one evening in the wake of an unexplained argument. "Just a great big hole to fill with their hate." Later, looking into her father's implacable face, a cold feeling tremored straight through to her toes. Dawn never knew what was happening behind that face—how close he was to a smile, or to a knife in your heart.

Dawn pounded the hood of the car with a fist. Dammit, she had to do something—something other than stand on the shoulder of this traffic-less road and soak the pavement with her childish tears. Reaching into the backseat, she grabbed the gift and wine (the dip would be the evening's casualty) and began walking toward a lone streetlight in the distance. Perhaps something was there—a diner, a roadside dive—and she could phone Rick. Joe or Damon would drive him here, so he could figure out what was wrong. He would be angry, to be sure, and hold it against her tomorrow—change his mind about disappearing for the evening and blare country tunes from the basement or jam the VCR so it could not be used—but what could she do . . . except, possibly (and her shoulders bunched at the thought), she could call a tow truck—take care of matters on her own. There might be additional expense involved, but perhaps that would less likely draw Rick's ire. At the very least, his poker game could continue uninterrupted.

There was a sudden rustling in the trees, followed by dark splotches on the pavement. Soon, rain was plinking down around her. "Oh shit, oh shit, oh shit," Dawn muttered, picking up the pace, her ankles bending in the soft, uneven slope, the wine slipping through her arms. The road opened ahead, and Dawn jogged into the gravel drive of Dale Seitz's automotive repair, where a plastic sign laconically explained: "If It Broke, We Fix It." She darted under the awning, and surveyed the lot: no pay phone. Gusts of wind brought rain sideways, spattering her clothes and face, forcing her to turn away—toward the door. At this hour, the place had to be closed; however, if she could somehow get inside, there would have to be a phone. It crossed her mind to take this bottle of Chardonnay and heave it through the window, but that action was so contrary to anything she'd ever done—anything that anyone could ever imagine her doing—that she shook with fear for even thinking it. There was also, of course, the door. Surprisingly, it drifted back at her touch, banging against the inside wall like a person passing out. With soaked blouse and straggly hair, Dawn edged into an alien world filled with disheveled stacks of sports magazines, tiny pyramids of oil and transmission fluid, a bulky television set with knobs. On the wall behind the desk was a woman in lingerie, copious breasts spilling out over the first week of August. Dawn was struck by the smell of oil, burnt coffee, and fast food—the smell, in other words, of men.

After calling a tow truck (it would be an hour), she plopped down next to a donut sitting on a folding chair. She leaned over to admire the cool, perfect glaze. It made her smile. There's a donut in this room, she thought. Nothing bad can happen.

Rain fired down on the aluminum awning. If only she had just gone straight to the shower, arrived on time, suffered through the awkwardness. She saw her father standing behind the counter, writing up an order, listing in long rectangular boxes all the things wrong with her character. Then the lecture: Dawn, I can't keep up with the things you do wrong. You're too much. The world goes this way and you go that way, just for kicks. You'll learn though, he'd finish cryptically, smacking the form with the back of his hand. Oh will you learn.

So sure enough she was learning, soaked and wet and sitting in a flimsy folding chair, missing a party because she simply turned left. She stood up and went to the gift on the counter. The cashier had not even wrapped it. Just tied ribbon around the gold box. Dawn slid off the ribbon and removed the cover, which was soft from rain. Underneath the noisy tissue lay the red chemise—silent, demure. She rubbed the material between thumb and fingers, gently pressed the tiny hearts that ringed the neckline. She took it out, shook it down, danced it in front of her eyes, placed it against her body. Her last boyfriend broke up with her about her looks. "Don't get me wrong," he said, "you're pretty . . . but you don't get me going the way other women do."

Looking down at the undulating waves of silk, she thought, what did he know? What, for that matter, did any of them know? One after the other slipped into her life with the sole purpose of judging her and, in the space of a few months, finding her wanting. Was Rick any different? She thought of impending fall and winter—of long, dark, weeknight evenings at home, the television doing its best to make her laugh; the leafless maple in the front yard, the wind frightening the glass in its panes; and Rick snorting on the sofa, beat from another double shift. Perhaps what made him better was just that he lacked energy. Perhaps his relative goodness was nothing more than inertia.

The rain was slamming down now, like heavy, lethal fists. Dawn caught up the nightshirt and placed it over her head, sliding it over blouse and skirt. She felt awkward, hopeless—like always. Awkward in the heels Rick always demanded she wear; in the kitchen with meals that failed to cohere; in the bedroom, not knowing what moves to make, nor knowing how to mask displeasure at the moves made upon her. This morning in the center, while filing client folders, her bra had come undone and two heavy lumps of flesh slumped into her blouse. Standing in front of the bathroom mirror with a safety pin, she'd thought, my god, this is the epitome of my life.

Dawn reached behind, under the nightshirt, found the zipper to her soaking skirt and gave it a tug. It caught on the material as it always did and for a moment—looking out into the empty lot bathed in streetlight—she nearly lost her nerve. Then spying the donut on the chair, she laughed out loud and gave one good yank. Moving her hips a few times was enough to get the skirt to the floor. Pressing her hands against her thighs, she smoothed down the nightie like she was frosting a birthday cake. There. There! Now how better was that?

As Dawn turned to the mirror, she found herself looking

at a dark object—a smooth, cylindrical something that caused a prickly wash to course down her back, an acid heat not even silk could cool. Her head froze in half turn as she heard a voice, higher than expected, but too weak to break through the senseproof field of fear that had grown around her. Then, if the sweat beading like hot oil on her skin were any indication, there must have been a melting. That along with the fact that the words seemed to sharpen, becoming "What is this?" before giving way to unformed sound again, this time not words but laughter and the laughter was, like the voice, an octave higher than she might have thought had she had time to think, and soon, as the heat turned to cool drops on her lip, her back, her thighs, she was not afraid to look up and face the owner of the voice and laugh because this person was a woman.

Traces of acne canvassed the woman's face, giving contour to her banged forehead. When she smiled again, Dawn half-expected braces.

"Are you trying to get killed?" The gun was no longer pointing.

Dawn flounced the nightshirt, felt the red seeping into her face. "It's a long story," she said, wondering where to begin, wondering how to get from that beginning to the end— here in an automotive shop, prancing around in someone else's nightie, staring down the barrel of a gun. But really it wasn't a story—just an accidental chain of events. Nothing she said could make sense. Or could it? As she looked harder, closer, at the woman, she suddenly recognized her, had seen her somewhere in town, at Hangover's or the QuikPik or . . . at New Start, that was it! This poor woman shuffled in some months ago, on a soggy spring day, with only a shopping bag of underwear. Her husband, she'd told one of the counselors, had not just kicked her out of the house, he beat her out of it. She had the blue arms and face to prove it. Dawn, making photocopies by the open office door, had seen her heaving in the chair, crying without tears.

But there was more to remember about her. There was her name—the name she'd heard the counselor speak before saying it was all going to be okay, the name she heard sometime later when the counselor had said "I'm so so happy for you." She glanced at the woman's uniform and sure enough: "Dawn." D-A-W-N in cheery red cursive.

"Are you Dawn? Are you?"

The woman peered, like she was trying to see her reflection in the window of a darkened room. Her pupils opened with fear and her grip on the weapon instinctively tightened. Then she understood, and the dark pools of her eyes receded.

Dawn nonchalantly brought her arms across her breasts, but she was shaking, from the chill, from the sudden realization of a gun barrel inches from her now convulsing breasts. Her teeth began to chatter, and her skin seemed to rise away from her bones. It was coming off, or taking off, and there were tears too, warm rivulets of shame and joy combined, coursing toward her mouth like potent drops of medicine.

"Can . . . you . . ." she sputtered at last, trying like crazy to be still, "you . . . can you help?"

***

Dawn was home by one, just when Rick told her to be. He and the boys were still at it—their voices, loud from alcohol, leaping up the stairs at the most unexpected moments, as she stood over the sink scraping crud from the plates that held their microwaved snacks. Rick must have heard her arrive, for he said, "Last hand boys." Someone sounding like Joe was bragging about the "three sweet bitches" that were going to save his otherwise unlucky night. Talk like that normally made her wince; tonight, though, the crude words hardly touched her. Dawn was giddy, the tickle of laughter rising in her throat. A moment later, when she cut herself on a knife, she watched the blood drip into pristine suds. She could have died tonight. Had she made one wrong move—one sudden turn—a cool, smooth shell would have bored through her heart, splashed hot wet blood against her chest. God, the thought of that was strangely sweet and pure. It was almost like a fresh start—like falling in love.

Exquisite Alarm

Three revolutions usually serve, and here comes the coffee table again when you catch your breath to say we're just like a clock, two interlocked hands spinning across the face of our flesh colored carpet, and thumping toward exquisite alarm . . . only since I list endearingly to right, we're really dialing backwards. This is some consolation, I concede, but not enough for now, the tick tock morning of my fortieth year.

So to say you're sorry, you reach back into your time-honored bag of tricks, and I know the suit of the card long before the soft slow slide from the deck, long before the jubilant flip and slap, long before you even ask: That feel good? And that?

Of course, of course. Still, all this ticking has got me out of sorts. Here in our blinded living room is the soft, warm present fact of you, yet as we fly, propelled by beats of wax winged hearts, I can't keep focused on the love at hand. Damn those neighbor kids, so new, so young, so screaming in the drive—the across the street boy, the next door girl, the splashings in her plastic pool. Together now, the boy implores, and then in the unbearable leap of silence before the splash, I see them dry as baby powder, jumping from a craggy perch, their long, awkward tumble through air, hearts pounding through breastbones as eyes grow equal to their fate, and I hear the hard crack of water that kick starts me back to you, me—us in our morning dusk, in the middle of our lives, spinning and spinning through some strange marriage of now and then and now I'm quickly close, so close I have to clench my teeth, ball my fists together, count to seven, and eight, and nine and when all that might not work, I conjure up the things that give me pause: the cold, implacable fact of forty—the dry and wrinkled end to all my timing.

I fall back into the heart of our lovelorn couch, unspent as a personal day. You lie there smooth and white, blinking with incredulity. For twenty years I've wandered—in and out and in and out toward something that always left me dead as suicides on rocks below. But this time—this one and only time perhaps—I've come out with my life intact. Hear it in my back to normal breaths. Feel it in the prickling of my sweating skin. See it in the bulging of my eyes that stare beyond the cutlery of our blinds, out there, where the revolutions of morning blur, out there, where everything is coming—and I mean everything . . . in one back winding dive towards birth.

Bounce the Ball

This kid Bill we can never get rid of, this kid when no one's home walks back and forth on the tree lawn, some dumb tennis game of his own, and when we pull in the drive last night, he bounds across the street, a pudgy boy in a crew cut, his dad back at the mental hospital, his mom sleeping around the neighborhood and neither too jazzed about having brought him into the world, since surprise surprise he's not a toy but a human being you actually have to give a shit about, and tonight, Bill's got this great red Martian head of a ball, which he must have found because his parents aren't givers, Christ, for supper they usually hand him hotdogs right from the fridge, processed cheese food fresh from the wrapper.

He's excited, he's just a water balloon of excitement this Bill, calling out "Ray, Ray, Ray…" and we're not even out of the minivan, tired from the trip to see my family, which has gone as well as a funeral on a sunny summer day, and all the way home Ray's whining about his Game Boy on the fritz and, almost home, he starts in about how we should pick up Toggle at the kennel now instead of in the morning, just so he can piss on the carpet because they locked him in a cage all day—piss and bare his teeth like Joanna, bitching because we didn't stop on the turnpike for supper, even though the food's all crap and she'll be complaining later about heartburn or gas, and I'm thinking this is what we'll have until Ray grows up—this bothersome Bill bouncing a ball in our drive—until Ray grows up, meets the wrong kids, gets his tattoo and develops his serial killer swagger, grabs Bill by his fuzzy head, and tells him to go to hell, and, speaking of hell, there's work, bet my email account's about ready to explode, so much to catch up on it will be Friday until I breathe, unless Jerri's already got that next project on my desk and then I'm screwed like a bachelor party whore, damn these ambitious women who have to climb out of their hole by stuffing you back in yours, and how long will it be until Ray has his nude girl etched into his arm? Eight years? Ten? A sharp pain soars to the center of my head and screams.

"Ray, Ray, Ray," Bill's like a goddamn broken toy, and I should know because Joanna buys him enough of them, the junk that's in that boy's room, he plays with something five minutes maybe ten—the best thing in the world—and then it's on to yammering about what else he wants, and now my head's nearly splitting, I see both halves dropping to the asphalt like cantaloupe.

"Ray, Ray, Ray . . ."

Either I adopt him or I want him out of the yard, it's what I've told Joanna from the beginning, I'm not callous, I just would rather establish a clear, definitive relation, better than this barnacling to us every time we come home or Christ go outside, we can't even enjoy a little peaceful backyard barbecue time on Sunday without Bill's fat head dropping over the fence like a tear that won't fall, and what are we going to do, I mean I'd be happy to say not today, but Joanna's up opening the gate, letting the boy in, goddamn it what's with women, they have this thing with children, just accept them one is the same as another, zero ability for discernment.

"How bout we play bounce the ball?"

Bounce the ball is the game he wants to play, the thing that can't even wait until we're out of the van and unpacked and enjoying a breath or two in the house we haven't seen these last two weeks, and he wants to play bounce the fucking ball, Christ, if I had suggested such a thing when I was young and shit my head it hurts, I know it's just exhaustion and hunger and maybe we should have stopped for food, why was I in such a hurry to get home, to enjoy a few moments of peace in the place where I'm said to live even though everyone knows I really live in a ten by ten cubicle with a computer and cold cups of Styrofoam coffee, and bagel crumbs, and this is my life, my real life, and man I'm just tired of running and thinking and meeting and living life like an unending sentence, I mean my brain, sometimes I imagine it with a tongue out, panting, out of breath, and that's probably why when the kid says bounce the ball I want to laugh and that's probably why, actually I don't know why, but it hits me like a Christmas bonus when Joanna's dragging the suitcases up the stairs, maybe something about adults turning away from the tragedy of youth or some such crap, but that boy's whole life spreads out in front of me like the soft carpet in our TV room, where evenings I lie in the cool pool of air conditioning and watch baseball games while Ray drives Matchbox cars all over me, and what I'm thinking is there's something good about "How bout we play bounce the ball," while Joanna's in the house already and Ray is on the stairs, eyes back in his video game, ears deaf to Bill's idea, which is something so good and simple and stunning, it makes me think I could love, yes I could love this kid. I could just slow down. I could play his goddamn game. I could be a better person. There still is time.

FOUR

August Is Young

It was one of those pleasant and lazy days before we acknowledged the need for divorce. I sat on the porch swing, cross-legged, a warm mug of coffee insulating me from unseasonable chill. A nervous sparrow cracked seeds on the ledge of the feeder. The girl across the street—her name is Trace—bounded down the stairs, a purple back-pack bouncing against her shoulder blades. A Chevy crept by, Nate Block's father tossing news onto dewy lawns. David Sorely—recently retired and widowed—appeared in the drive, nose white with sunscreen, a fishing hat flop-ping over his head. He gave a salutary snip with clippers before beginning the careful pruning of front lawn hedges.

My wife came out with coffee pot in hand, lustrous hair channeled over a shoulder, a smile like brittle crust over a wound. The dark liquid sloshed like the ocean we'd never seen until last summer. Our first night was in Plymouth— an inn on the rocks and then the ocean, the awesome endless loop of waves. She was smiling then, and my heart was afloat, like the dirty gull motionless in the distance, hovering as if that one place and time above the sea were good enough forever.

Then my wife was in the kitchen, butter coming to life in the pan. Fresh, cool air sighed through the screened-in porch. It was August third, I think—or some day young enough in the month to make me smile for all the good days left to summer, all the good moments like those that come so slowly now, like deep deliberate breaths—the kind the doctor asks for.

God She Could Tolerate

"The Lord is good," John declared, his voice tumbling from the shadows at the top of the stairs.

Maddy, squinting up at the crimson tie John had been looking for all morning, wished like hell he could have just said "God." God, after all, she could tolerate. If nothing else, the word still carried rhetorical power as the prefix of powerful expletives. But "Lord"—and especially the way John *intoned* it—made Maddy shudder. John was her life partner, her significant other, whom she'd chosen for his wit, his cool, incisive mind. Yet here he was this morning, sounding like some Southern fried Jesus freak who might at any moment crash to the floor and start babbling in tongues.

"Gruyère is good," Maddy said, trying to make light of situation. "Cheval Blanc."

John disappeared with a flat-lipped smile into the bedroom. Maddy slumped at the kitchen table for the next ten minutes, picking at a three day old bran muffin and wondering how she would endure this man's hairpin curve back to the church. She knew this much for sure: She'd die if he came back downstairs with a goddamn bible tucked underneath his arm.

John and Maddy had been in one school or another for as long as they could remember. Through luck and ambition (or "Providence," as John would probably have to have it now), they managed to secure a joint position at a prestigious university—Research One. John had been awarded tenure the year before, and now Maddy's promotion was a mere form letter from the president away. A dream come true, except for the fact that tenure meant "life" in north central Indiana—what she called her "maximum *obscurity* prison." She'd grown up in Philadelphia, which was certainly no great prize, but the city was infinitely superior to this dull, unleavened nowhere. As much as they could in the summers, she and John escaped the servile flatness, the soaring tentacles of corn, and the ubiquitous sickly smell of the corn syrup plant for the relative pleasures of her hometown: Bach or Beethoven at the Kimmel Center, an evening stroll through Rittenhouse Square, a long, late dessert at Lacroix. Freed from flyover country, she could even find pleasurable a slice of well-aged parmesan amid the frenzied squalor of Ninth and Christian. The city, what she liked to call its "raz and bristle"—that was the only thing that mattered. They'd train up to New York as often as possible, which was where Maddy always thought that people like her deserved to be. Among good friends, jealous but biting her tongue, she devoured small plates and martinis and off-Broadway shows and suddenly there was August, a fat and sweaty parole officer, casting its huge shadow over her, barreling onto the scene to cuff her and send her away all over again. There was the quiet flight back, the brooding shuttle ride through the land of corn and soybeans toward their home. With each passing year, an ink blot of anger grew in Maddy's stomach, coaxed along by John's seeming contentment with where they'd come to be.

On the way to church (Thank God there'd been no bible under John's arm!), she kept telling herself that this was normal. Plenty of people did such things—especially on Easter, when (as her father liked to say), "The cockroaches pour into the kitchen." Amazingly, a few of these churchgoing types could still be found in the academy. Back in February, for example, she saw ashes on the forehead of this stout, long-time adjunct whose name she could never remember. How embarrassed Maddy had been for her!

"Luke tells us the following," the suave, pomaded priest explained during the homily. "'They found the stone rolled away from the tomb; but when the apostles entered, they did not find the body of the Lord Jesus.'" He stepped down into the congregation, this thin, toothy, well-groomed man. With both hands, Maddy clutched the seat of the pew.

"Imagine," he continued, hands flung from his vestments as if he were casting a spell. "Just *imagine* their surprise. The rise—the *electric charge*—those men must have felt as the beam of truth shot through them."

Two rows in front of them, a mother had been trying for

some time to get a little girl to sit down in the pew. The girl cried, "You can't make me!"

"God works in mysterious ways," the priest said, as if this had been a scripted part of the act.

Maddy bowed her head to the chuckles and guffaws. The inkblot grew, seemed to seep out of her stomach and wisp like smoke into the rest of her body. Instinctively, she put her hands to her abdomen. John, looming over her with big, brown eyes, wondered if everything was okay.

***

"I don't . . . *wish* to criticize," she said as John turned out of the church lot. "But what a . . . a tawdry performance!" She made him a list: slick priest, hand holding during the Lord's Prayer, saccharine hymns, florid piano playing, bongos. "Bongos, John! For the love of God!"

"Do you know what I think?" John asked.

"I forgot," she said. "Why don't you give it to me in a parable?"

"I don't appreciate your tone."

"Oh, tell me!" She slapped him on the knee. Somewhere, she'd seen young women do this when they wanted to be "playful."

At the light, John turned to her and smiled, one lip firm against the other. Maddy could lecture quite eloquently on Kristeva and the semiotic, she could explain *différance* so well that her students left class brooding about the utter incompetence of the language they believed to be their own. But for all her intellect, all her training, Maddy no longer had a clue about this man behind the wheel. Was his smile a sign of professorial condescension? Subtle derision? Genuine spiritual contentment? Maddy did not—Maddy *could not*—believe in a John without irony.

To her surprise, John drove right past their house and turned left on Route 26. Soon they were approaching the strip mall world out by the interstate. Refusing to ask the question she knew he wanted her to ask, Maddy stared at the white splotch of bird shit on the windshield until it reminded her of communion, the wafer fixed against the roof of her mouth. All the way back to the pew, she'd worked her tongue against it, trying to pry the damn thing loose.

"Do you wonder where we're going?" John asked, his tone easy and pleasant.

She shrugged her shoulders.

"I have reservations."

So they were going to brunch, which perhaps was her reward for humoring him on this Easter morning. They drove past restaurant and hotel chains on either side of the straight flat road that always seemed to Maddy like the visual representation of the imagination running out of gas. And this was the place she had to call home: Lafayette—or "Laff-at-it," as her clever graduate students liked to say.

"What a beautiful afternoon!" John said, apropos of nothing.

At least he didn't say "Lord." He didn't say the Lord had

anything to do with it, so for that reason Maddy decided that she could tentatively accept the proposition, even if it stunk a bit of sentimentality. To be charitable, to show that there were no hard feelings, she was even going to say "indeed"; but then, the silly fool, he kept on going. "Forty years," he said, turning to her with moist, dung-like eyes. "I don't think I have ever taken the time . . ."

All at once, the ink shot up Maddy's throat, dark and sticky, something even a hellish round of coughing could not expel.

"Are you . . . Dear? What's the matter?"

"I'm fine," she said, although she really wanted to scream "Shut up!" because John, poor vapid John, was beginning to sound exactly like a deathbed scene from one of those Victorian novels he loved to teach. Soon, he'd be maudlin about most everything—blossoms on a cherry tree, a nephew's gap-toothed smile, a *Lifetime* movie at the holidays. He'd never let up about God's gifts, his abiding grace, and all of that tripe. In the coming days, John was going to be insufferable.

He pulled into the packed lot of a popular family restaurant, "Home of the Biscuit-n-Gravy Challenge." Awaiting them was food not unlike a set of term papers: bland, unimaginative, indigestible with their long, terrible sentences that made her want to stamp NO NO NO—one thick black word per page.

"We have arrived," John said, gently shifting to park.

As Maddy released her seatbelt, the sky suddenly darkened. In Cleveland, a place she despised every single moment of her undergraduate career, there was this Oldenburg sculpture, a huge rubber stamp that shouted the word FREE. The thing rested on its side on the City Hall lawn, looking like it had just dropped from the sky. Maddy winced. She didn't have to look up to know that the shadow was Indiana's own special state stamp, here once but coming now again, plunging toward this flat paper world for emphasis, to better pronounce the contour of the words that had made their mark upon them both.

The Please Pitch

The form was pink, amorphous, something resembling the outline around a shot dead body.

"That's Clara," Hillary said, pointing with a stubby finger of chalk. "She's my best friend."

Jim Mornette shared a driveway with the Whites, and this meant he shared (much to his chagrin) their six-year old daughter as well. The cracked ramp of asphalt was her playground. She was playing hopscotch in her school uniform when he left for work in the morning and twirling on her scooter when he returned at night. Often in the six weeks since he moved here, he had to stand in the drive, listening to this girl go on about the horrors of pepperoni pizza day at school (she picked them off), or the centipede she nearly stepped on in their basement recreation room, or any number of kiddie TV shows, this Uncle Fuzzy for example, about a sentient speck of dust skittering around someone's unkempt home.

But this morning, he had no time to humor her. Mornette had had a torturous night, awakened at one in the morning by a lone woman's voice down the street. Then, inevitably, a series of memories like late model sports cars roared through his head, keeping him awake until three-thirty or four, when he plunged so deep off the edge of consciousness he was running a half hour late by the time the radio alarm finally reached him.

Placating Hillary with a quick series of nods, he fell into his Focus, locked the door, and crammed the key in the ignition. Hillary pressed her face against the window.

"Move," he mouthed, flicking his fingers at the glass in case she didn't understand.

Mornette didn't hear the screams until he was halfway down the drive. After the first moment of blind petrifaction, he realized the sound was not coming from underneath the tires, but from the stairs next door, where Hillary now stood, mouth open, tiny arm thrusting at the asphalt.

"What's wrong?" he asked, rolling down the window.

But Hillary was already up the stairs and into the house, her next shriek muffled by the screen door slapping shut. By the time she and her mother returned to the porch, Mornette was out of the car, looking under the wheels for the cat he must have creamed. When Mrs. White appeared on the porch next door, Mornette shrugged his shoulders.

"Your little girl just started screaming."

"It's her friend, the drawing," she said matter-of-factly. "You ran her over."

Mornette had only ever seen Mrs. White for brief moments—flopping out in slippers for the paper, tossing old bread onto the back lawn for the birds, taking off in mismatched clothes for a brief weekend jog. Now, with the young sun ruthless on her face, she struck him as much older than her age, which he figured to be early thirties. Well, he thought, a poorly cauterized anger opening up within him, she deserved it. Accelerated aging was apt comeuppance for this temperamental child.

"You *killed* her," Hillary shouted, a wedge of angry face slicing out from behind the mother's hips.

Mornette made the appropriate—the neighborly— apologies, but inside, somewhere back beyond an encroaching headache, a counterforce was gathering, something powerful and soothing that was jetting out a message toward his lips to smile. He had to cough into a hand to cover it up.

***

Mornette was late for work, but the showroom was a cemetery, the shiny sedans and trucks like so many garish headstones. A few people wandered the outside lot for awhile, but scurried away upon his smiling approach. Late in the afternoon, however, against all probability, Mornette managed to sell a brand new fully loaded Escape to a family planning a cross-country vacation. The husband was ready to buy the second he sat behind the wheel and the two polite (and, as the husband bragged, home schooled) kids were all for it when they saw *Finding Nemo* running on the DVD player. The woman, however, after a series of frowns, walked to the other side of the showroom to examine some of the more economical sedans, a ream of Internet printouts cradled in her arms.

"Tell you what," Mornette said, when he finally coaxed husband and wife back to his desk. "Here are the keys. Take it for a drive. Talk about it. I'll hold the fort." He even pulled out the magic jar from the bottom drawer so the kids could choose a miniature candy bar or two. Twenty minutes later, the couple returned, the wife biting her lip and thrusting a piece of paper at him. "This is the monthly we can afford. Make it happen." He hadn't noticed before, but this woman had Linda's nose, or at least the thin-skinned shiny bridge of it. Words failed him only for a moment, until he found the power to forgive the accidental resemblance—forgive it thoroughly and beautifully for the sake of the commission, forgive it with his most disarming grin and, fresh from a quick consultation with his manager, the confident, stock phrase he used with them all: "You just bought yourself a brand new bouncing baby Ford." By the time all the papers were signed, Mornette's migraine was gone, the husband and his Linda-nosed wife held hands, and the boy and girl danced wildly with the promise of a fast food supper.

***

When he arrived home, Mornette noticed a parking space directly in front of his house. He thought about pulling in the drive, murdering again Hillary's chalk blob of a friend. Three hours ago, that would have seemed to him the perfect way to end the day. But now, the thought of a nice tidy commission gave him pause. He could always pull the car in later, after the young girl went to bed. And in the morning? Well, he'd think of something. Perhaps he could bend over and politely ask Clara to move. Or he could kindly ask Hillary to redraw the friend on her side of the drive. He was not a bad man, given the right conditions.

Walking up the drive, Mornette saw that Clara had been redrawn. Not only was she darker—more defined—around the edges, she now possessed clear facial features: sad, parabolic eyes, a nose like a paper clip, a mouth jagged as a mountain road. Stepping carefully around the resurrected friend, Mornette noticed Hillary lurking at her kitchen window, the translucent curtain pulled tightly against her face.

"Don't do that. You're going to suffocate."

Hillary closed her eyes. Mornette read this as willful disdain.

"Do you want to kill yourself?"

Her nodding face—up and down against the curtain—made a sound like nervous slicing.

***

His microwaved dinner was cold in spots, but Mornette, who'd only had a few sandwich cookies for lunch, was too ravenous to care. He brought the soft cardboard box of food to the living room, where he sat down with modest anticipation, clicked the remote, only to see silver blue snow shaking across the screen. How could he forget that the cable was still out?

He blew on a flaccid tree of sauce-covered broccoli and stuck it in his mouth, listening to the hitch in his jaw as he chewed, his mind scuttling back to last August when he made that popping sound and Linda told him to "Please be quiet"—this at a posh lakefront restaurant in Marblehead shortly before the end, as if he were not innocently eating his crab cakes but blabbing on about annoying customers or intestinal gas. Embarrassed, he remembered slowly turning his eyes to her, studying the skin burnished from the tanning salon, the sunset colored dress clinging to her sturdy form. And her nose—compact, slightly rounded, the bridge polished like a fine piece of furniture. On any other woman, that nose would have been cause for acute self-consciousness. On Linda, it was her crowning glory.

"Can't you control it?" she asked.

"I've got really good command of my ears. Maybe I could eat through them."

Her laugh was one part mirth, two parts derision. Lately, she'd been playing fast and loose with that recipe, and the result was a concoction that was becoming more venomous by the day.

They'd been dating for years, on and off for much of the time, in the desultory fashion of those with eyes furtively scanning the horizon for something better. In the last year, though, they had become exclusive—"committed," as Linda put it once, although there was something in the shape of her eyebrow that reminded him of a question mark.

It was because he'd known her for so long that he had taken the restaurant scolding in stride. Later that evening, he even seemed to think it registered a deeper level of intimacy.

That fall, with big plans looming in his head, he booked a room at a lodge in Grant National Forest, opting for the "Honeymoon Special" on a whim, since it came with champagne and chocolate and a heart-shaped hot tub in the room . . . and since it might put her in the mood to receive the ring he'd bought her six months before.

The weekend was unseasonably cold—in the upper 30s, with a chance of flurries. Shortly after they arrived the first day, they hiked for an hour, up what the lodge brochure had called a "moderately difficult" path through the Appalachian foothills, until Linda tripped over yet another tree root and stopped in her tracks, saying her hands were just about ready to fall off. This seemed a typical exaggeration, but Mornette, wanting things to go smoothly, didn't press. He nodded, agreed, took one of those falling off hands, in fact, and led her safely back to the lodge. It was Saturday—just 3:30 in the afternoon— and Mornette found himself trying to figure out how to pry her out from the peevish mood she'd locked herself inside of. He decided on a small glass of port and a movie that began with a frenetic domestic scene—a young boy and girl fighting over the TV, a harried woman sketching lip liner across her mouth as she hard heels it down a hallway and bursts into the bedroom, hollering at them to stop, the girl stomping out, a man brushing by her going the other way, hands up and whining where are those goddamn papers?

"Brats," Linda murmured.

They watched in silence for about forty-five minutes before Mornette suddenly put the DVD player on pause.

"You mean to tell me," he said, thinking of the ring tucked in the sock pouch of his suitcase, "you don't ever really want one?"

"One what?"

"A child."

This was familiar territory, a "more than moderately difficult path" they'd hiked before—many, increasingly arduous times before. Just as on the trail a few hours earlier, Linda grew cold here—her pupils contracting, her lips losing shape, her arms drawing around her body. "Jim. Really. What do you want me to say?"

Mornette stared at the frozen TV screen. The man who had been running around for his important papers looked much different now, his slick grey suit torn and blood spattered, his pomaded hair now wild with perspiration, his mouth hanging open. His day had started out like any other, but now he found himself staring down from a bridge into a violent, rocky rush of water. Mornette recalled having seen the film before. This man was going to jump. He had to, in order to escape his pursuers, in order to make it back to his family, the kids he said he loved in the tear-jerking scene the minute before.

"I want you to say, 'I am a woman. Of course I want to have a child.'"

"I have a career," she said with a cavalier slap to her jeans. "A very fulfilling career."

"You've been saying this for years."

"This is what *I* want right now."

"But you're thirty-five."

"So?"

"You're a goddamn grade school teacher!"

Mornette hoped he'd struck a blow—something hard and deep that might crack open the hard, protective shell and release her warm and flowing instinct for maternity. But Linda only laughed—a strident and judgmental laugh.

"You don't respect my job? *You*? The shady car salesman?"

Before Mornette could defend himself, Linda's cell phone went off—a maddeningly electronic Beethoven's Fifth. He watched her work frantically at the buttons to shut it off. Mornette pressed play on the remote and the man leapt, his suit fluttering up around his shoulders like wings. Linda got up and padded toward the bathroom, leaving the phone on the middle cushion of the sofa, where it sat like a giant black beetle. He half expected it to crawl away.

***

The next day, Mornette woke to the sound of rain on the awnings, his throat dry, and his eyes swimming with allergy. The public radio station was laying it on thick with groaning cellos and weepy violas. The melody made him angry. He sneezed his way through a shower, started to get dressed, and then, after hearing the lousy weather report for a third time, fell back onto his bed and reached for the phone. On a day like this, he could not bear the thought of work.

An hour later, when the rain let up a bit, Mornette darted out to the end of the drive to retrieve his paper. On the way back, he met Hillary bouncing down the stairs, her face distorted under the translucent umbrella.

"Today is Clara's birthday," she said. "She is one, two, three, four—four days old."

Only the faintest traces of the imaginary friend clung to the asphalt.

"I killed Clara," Mornette said. "I ran her over."

"What you did? That was just death for a while."

"And now she's drowned in the rain."

"She's just going away to get ready."

Hillary stood smug under her umbrella while Mornette's teeth ground behind soldered lips.

"You know, once you're dead, you're dead. It's a one time thing."

He desperately wanted the girl to cry, but she just looked up at him through the umbrella, the same superior smile on her face, more firmly set now that she came to the realization—whether conscious or not—that she had beaten this man at something significant, the victory underscored by the fact that he was getting soaked while she was dry from head to toe.

So he slapped her hard, not across the face (the umbrella was in the way) but on the baby fat of her arm. At first, he thought Hillary hadn't even noticed. She was so still—no cry, no dropped open mouth, no plinking tears. He looked down through the umbrella for some kind of response, but all he saw were eyes, large, direct, and frozen solid behind the plastic.

Shirt clinging to his skin, Mornette retreated to his house and slammed the door.

He pulled down the shade of the window facing his drive and took the paper out of its plastic bag. On the front page was the story of an earthquake in some city Mornette would never be able to locate on the map. It was no longer a rescue mission. The searchers had switched to full recovery mode. Yet just this morning they had heard a tinking under the rubble. Was it possible someone was still alive, ten days after the disaster? When did the workers just start rubbing dirt and tears from their eyes and mumble, "I give up"?

His cell phone sounded. At first, he figured Mrs. White was calling to say how dare you touch my child, for Hillary seemed the kind of girl to give full and immediate report. Mrs. White would call the police, and he would be taken out of the house in cuffs. Before they came, he'd get in her face, tell her that Hillary was no innocent child, that she was precocious in her diabolism . . . . But this was his business line, and there was no good reason why Mrs. White would have the number. On the fourth ring, he chanced a pick up.

"This is Debbie Torelli."

It took Mornette a moment to recall the name—place it on that woman with the Linda nose who bought the decked out Explorer. He braced himself for complaint.

"I wanted to thank you in person . . .well, not in person, but over the phone."

"Thank me?"

"You were so patient with us, me especially. I've been burned a few times, so I might have come on strong."

Mornette was speechless.

"Anyway, we love it. I took it out on the highway this morning. It handles so well."

"I'm glad."

"You probably don't get many of these calls." Again that laughter.

"Tell my manager."

"He's next on my list."

"I was kidding."

"Seriously."

"That's kind of you."

"I'll recommend you to my friends."

Mornette hung up and wandered from living room to dining room to kitchen and back again before climbing the stairs and lying back down on his bed. It was the dazed feeling of the infatuated—exacerbated by the effects of allergy medicine, perhaps, but that's what it was, like in those early days with Linda when neither knew enough about the other to stay the hell away, when he was smitten as much by her physical beauty as by her idealism, teaching children because she "truly and dearly" loved every last one of them. Parents of these children, her own relatives, and just about everyone else she came in contact with wondered why she wasn't a mom already, and several times over. Linda was always polite with these people, her face darkening with a deferential blush that allowed her to avoid answering at the same time it left her inquisitors completely satisfied.

Mornette closed his eyes, but he was wide awake, unusually alert to the sniffling of his nose, the birds in the maple outside the window, a lawn mower blaring down the street. Then all at once he was crying. He was thirty-six and his parents were dead, his closest friends had long since deserted him for either coast. He had not a single soul to love him. He was a man who like all the men he knew steeled himself against the pusillanimous shame of tears. Now, he did not care. He was going to take all the time he needed—the whole day, if necessary—to feel sorry for himself.

***

The next morning was brilliant with sun. Hillary sat cross-legged in the drive, directly behind his car, in the middle of some strange figure chalked out in red.

"And who might this be?"

"This," she said sweeping her arms around in a circle, "is you."

He didn't like the fact that he had no discernible shape.

"You'll have to move."

She started drawing facial features. He watched her in silence for a few moments, letting patience serve as a kind of apology. He let one minute then two go by, and then he picked her up. Gently. He made sure of this. He didn't want trouble. He put her out of the way. Turning back to his car, he saw that the front driver's side tire had melted into the drive. He kicked the side of the door.

Hillary said, "You can't go anywhere."

For the first time in days, Mornette saw her clearly. Her eyes were emerald disks floating above plump cheeks. Waiting eyes—without a trace of fear or anger or pain.

"Why did you do this?"

Hillary skipped into the red circle and started to tap, as if it were a spotlight.

"Answer me."

"Daddy is going to Columbus for awhile." She scuffled her shoes again. "To visit relatives. He's going to get well there too."

Mornette had seen Dale White only once. It was a late March evening, and Mornette had been sitting up in bed, waiting for Linda to leave his brain. He looked out the window into the White's backyard and saw Dale in the glow of a portable grill. He was seasoning something, flipping it—a steak, perhaps. He was slipping it off the grill onto a plate. He was sitting down at the table to eat. His shirt was off. He sat on the pink, plastic picnic table Hillary used for her dolls. Mornette watched his back, the pale curve of his shoulders, and listened to the fork and knife skitter across the plate.

Mornette opened the trunk and unfastened the jack. He stood again before her.

"Hold out your hands."

She did. They were so small, intriguing in their delicacy. He placed the jack into her hands.

"You're helping me," he said, gesturing vaguely behind him. "I need you to help me fix this."

Hillary blinked. Her squat nose jumped. Once, when he first started working for the dealership—this was, what? maybe thirteen fourteen years ago—he was trying to sell a Mustang to a man who'd just gotten divorced. He was in the process of building up his life again, and the first piece of the edifice was to be a brand new car. But the guy was hedging, he was I don't knowing. Mornette, who'd been working a week without a sale, finally just said, "Take it for a spin. Please?" There must have been something in the desperation of his voice that trumped the grief of this newly single and lonely man, for he did take the car for a test drive, and one half hour later, the car was his. Mornette had the first sale of his career.

"Please?" he said.

She didn't move.

"You set it under the car," he explained, getting down on his knees to position the jack under the frame. "Then you put the little pole in like this." He looked back at her, standing now with folded grown up arms. "You can do it," he said.

She didn't move.

And then (who knows why?) she did: slowly, dragging her feet, just like anybody's obedient daughter.

Everything Off

It's a hard thing, and harder than usual this first full day alone, for Lee to leave his house—to walk, to *stride*, torture free, coat over shoulder, out the front door and into the almost negligent normality of a suburban Monday morning. It's hard on account of all or most of the things he owns, all the things just waiting for a moment's inattention to burn the place down—the toaster and the microwave, the TV and the lamps, the washer and dryer, the space heaters up and down, both of which he always, always places in the middle of his living room floor, plugs at forty five degrees from outlets just dying to be faulty.

It's so hard today that Lee makes it to work only after three false starts, each time a little further out the door before being dragged back to check what's been checked and checked again. He makes it to work, opens a bottle of water, logs into his computer, and review client files but all the while his brain is scrambling back to his house all big and old and utterly alone, his long time, work-at-home love, the mystery ghostwriter, no longer a fixture in the study by the stairs, no longer there to see or smell or feel if anything's amiss. He tries to work but finds himself thinking and thinking about the toaster and the microwave, the TV and the lamps, the washer and dryer, the space heaters up and down, until—just like that—he's thinking about the oven, the oven, the one thing that, despite all his caution, *may well* have slipped his mind. He thinks about that big sleek box filling up right now with gas—the gas wrapping invisible arms around a darling little spark, even though he thinks he knows (of course he knows!) the knob was pointing up when he gave it one good last stare this morning. He remembers (Doesn't he? Doesn't he?) the snap of the knob back in place at the *exact same moment* he whispered "Pillsbury" into the dark aperture of his fist.

***

The snap of the knob, the snap of the knob—or is Lee remembering the morning before, the snap of the knob at the *exact same time* his mystery writer, freshly showered and gorgeous in a black turtleneck, appeared in the archway of the kitchen, took a deep breath, and said, "You are too much."

"More is good," Lee sang, self-conscious in bathrobe and slippers, glad to have blueberry muffins, their customary breakfast in bed, to slide from the oven, glad for something warm and golden brown to rest his eyes on, glad if for no other reason than there was no chance he'd forget the snap of the knob when his mystery man went on to say, "We are over" because over was like oven and the oven was now off just like his mystery man who was off after packing and a few more painful parting words. He was off, out the door and off, just like they were off, which was not that far from over, which brought Lee back to oven, which reminded him of how free he was to leave the house on that gorgeous, sunsilly Sunday morning, even though he had nowhere he especially cared to go.

***

"Maybe if you lived in Centralia," his mystery man said one pleasantly cool fall evening a few weeks earlier, as they sat sipping martinis on the backyard patio.

Lee shrugged his shoulders.

"That old mining town, up by Harrisburg. It's been burning for forty something years. If you lived *there*, then I could see why you'd worry a bit about leaving your house."

Lee jammed his tongue against his upper teeth. He could afford a lavish smile because he was just four or five steps to everything—the toaster and the microwave, the TV and the lamps, the washer and dryer, the space heaters up and down. He smiled because his mystery man had finally lost the anger of the morning, when it took Lee forever to leave the house for a day trip to Rehoboth Beach, when he was frozen by the front door, eyes scrambling back into the rooms, reassuring himself of the unequivocal offness of everything—three minutes, four, or maybe ten spent in staring and checking and trying to mentally tick off all the things he could not see, while his lover fumed and honked, ticking them off (or trying to) so that nothing while they played and ate and loved might short or spark and burn their home to the ground.

"Where does it come from?" he wondered, placing his soft hand on Lee's. "Just give me a cause. You know, one reason. If I knew, maybe I wouldn't . . . maybe I could understand, you know?"

The caress of the question made Lee want so badly to fill the silence with an answer. He wanted to blame overprotective parents. He wanted to point a finger at the nuns, the ones who stalked up and down the rows and pinched your ears if you answered wrong. A beautiful boy who stuck him in the heart when his back was turned. His job—the unrelenting dullness of handling insurance claims. Was it all of these or none of these or every other one that was the cause?

His mystery man sat up for a response. He studied Lee with dark, wide, research-eager eyes.

***

Lee pushes the oven out of mind as best he can until one, at which time he discovers he's forgotten his lunch at home, right there on the bottom shelf of the refrigerator, the handled bag with the tofu salad sandwich, the carrot sticks, the lemon juiced apple wedges all in their separate plastic containers. He can almost see the bag, the shelf, the closed door, the fridge, the fridge, the fridge (the picture of it freezing in his mind), the fridge resting between the counter and the wall, warm to the touch and what if warm becomes hot and is the box of cereal too close and why did he leave that coupon under the magnet on the door, knowing that coupons, even for liquid soap, go straight into the credenza? He should know, he should because wasn't it just last week he'd read that article about "sneak up on you" fires—a laptop with a faulty battery that went up in flames inside the trunk of a car at the Granite Run Mall, a hot bedroom socket in a South Philly row that one day had enough. Lee can almost feel the fridge, feel it warming and glowing and roasting and how boiling must it get before it can catch cardboard or newspaper on fire while he sits fifteen miles away, listening to an angry client plead her hopeless case?

"But he said he wasn't even looking," the woman cries. "He told me while we waited for the cop!"

Not looking, not looking, not looking . . . while the old, overheating ivory giant in the hole between wall and countertop is getting ready to explode.

"Then the cop comes," the lady continues. "The cop comes and, oh, get this: The guy changes his tune, says *I* ran the stop sign—"

"According to the police report, there were no witnesses. The officer could not determine fault."

"Sir, I wasn't the one chomping on a hoagie while making a left hand turn!"

Lee has a phone right in his hand and another clipped to his belt, but there's no one to call, there's not one single person to let him know how dangerous everything has become. The woman is still talking, but he's fixated on the blank gray wall of his cubicle, which suddenly looks a lot like smoke. He sees the coupon on the refrigerator door curling brown before his eyes. He sees the house in flames, everything left now just a sizzling pile of ash.

Lee drops the phone, stands up, speeds down the corridor, conscious of curious faces rising above cubicle walls. His supervisor calls out, "Is everything . . . ?" but he doesn't hear the rest because he's in the stairwell and then out the door and at his car, cranking it over and bolting out of the lot, onto the Blue Route and in and out of midday traffic, holding his breath all the way home and into the terrible stillness of the kitchen. The first thing he does is rip the coupon from the fridge and place it in the credenza where it goes. He puts the box of cereal safely on the middle cushion of the living room sofa, far enough and strange enough away that he will remember when he goes back to work. It is a luxury, but he leans against the back door and risks a short sigh of relief.

***

Lee used to assign each appliance a series of numbers and log them in on dated note cards which he kept in a recipe box labeled "Favorites." The container came with him to work during the week, so he could verify the numbers at his leisure. One day, though, he left it behind, and in his panic called home five times throughout the day, asking if everything was fine. When he returned home, leaving ten minutes early because the panic had again begun to clutch at his throat, his mystery lover was in the kitchen, the recipe box like a square brain between his hands.

"I was going to surprise you," he said. "Make one of the old favorites."

"They're all so good," Lee said, his face full of fire.

That was when he started ripping, one card at a time, ripping each in two and four and then snowing the pieces across the porcelain tile.

The next morning, Lee's ghostwriter was a ghost for good.

***

As he stands at the door of his house, lunch in one hand, a cold knob in the other, eyes darting around yet again to see each and everything turned off and off and off, Lee thinks and thinks and thinks and maybe it's time for something new, something different enough from what he's doing and has done that will stand out in his mind at work.

Maybe he could just walk outside. Maybe he could just walk to the car. Maybe he could put the shifter into drive. Roll five hundred feet down Orange. Take a left onto State. Drive through town at exactly twenty-five miles an hour. A right onto Providence. A left onto Baltimore Pike. Merge onto 476. Just one single thing at a time, and he could record each key moment of the trip with his camera before moving on, building a chain of images from home to work, a link at every step of the way so that when in his panic he forgets, he can look, he can see, he can see every move that got him here and know for sure that every single thing is off.

Halfway down the sidewalk, Lee turns around, comes back, and looks through the front window for smoke. When that's not good enough, he shoves the key back in the lock and throws the door aside, stomps back in and unplugs the toaster and the microwave, the TV and the lamps, the washer and dryer, the space heaters up and down (which he plugs in again in order to unplug). Soon, he's back in the kitchen, where the oven's off, the oven's off, the oven's off. He grabs and shakes both racks to see if they're still cold, which or course they are, since he didn't even use the oven, the oven, the oven, this morning, this morning, this morning.

But what about the fridge? How could he have left the house for so many days on end without ever thinking such a thing could easily turn against him?

Because, because (why hasn't he thought of it before?), he has not been afraid enough—and not being afraid enough is just as good or bad as being careless. He needs to be better, sharper, more vigilant. He needs to recognize that fear is who he is and who he'll always be, deep down under the skin, beneath the vital organs, in the fist like tangles of his wiring. He must fear, fear, fear all the things that may well happen—all the losses and the breakups, the maladies diseases and untimely deaths—so that when the time comes, when real life catches up with his anxious imagination, maybe Lee will be ready to survive the surprise.

Lee places both hands on the fridge and dances it from between the counter and the wall. He squeezes in behind, lies down on the crumb-filled linoleum, and with a flash-light finds the plug and pulls. As the beam shines on the naked face of the outlet, he listens to the current of silence rush through the house. He's alone—there's no one to come by, pick him up, no one anymore to say everything will be fine—so it's easy for him to lose track of just how long he watches those fathomless eyes and that sad bullet hole of a mouth, which seems so awfully desperate for a kiss.

Daisy

Despite the cops at the corner, it gets worse and worse
on Daisy Avenue: music like fists, car windows punched,
teeth of seething dogs against chain link fences. "What are
you going to do?" my dad sighs over the phone, too old and
poor to leave.

Then: the corner store. For years, Mr. Jobrani had been a
good man—no money-no-problem, pay whenever you can.
Now he's just another of the dead. The ski masks left him on
the floor, bullets in the chest and head, blood sliding toward
the condiments. By the weekend, the masks were behind
bars, three doors down from where they lived.

Remember? That was the place for pretzel sticks—five
cents from a tin. Slim Jims. Baseball cards. We'd rip the
wrap for Indians, doomed already in June. One time, a
month after the perfect game, you found Len Barker and
made pink gum a tongue. "You wait," I cried, "You'll pay."

A week later, I asked Mr. Jobrani for the jelly gun on the
rack behind the counter. I pleaded, he frowned, but filled it
over the sink for free. I burst across the street as you, white
shirt for a christening, came down the drive. "So long,

sucker!" I cried. When you turned, I grinned, then shot a cherry stream to dye you.

FIVE

Opposites

The two year old opens her eyes. She says, "Mama up." She eats toasted oats and drinks juice cut with water from a sippy cup. She gnaws a strawberry. She flings the leafy stem onto the floor. She reads a book about a bear whose father comes home. She pours tea for a stuffed pig and a unicorn. She sits for awhile in a wicker basket. She hugs a can of black olives, which yesterday became her new best friend.

For lunch, she eats sliced turkey and garbanzos, cauliflower and apple sauce. She goes out back, breathes "oooh" upon a worm. She pulls out grass and lets it sail in the wind. She chalks three blue lines upon the sidewalk. "Bood," she says and flaps her wings. She climbs the ladder of her slide. She sits at the top. She slides down to the dirt and digs a hole in the ground. "Where Dada?" she says.

She sits in her high chair for supper. "Mama, Dada, baby, happay!" is her prayer. Afterward, she takes a bath. She cries when water spills over her soapy head. She takes a cup and gives her belly button a drink. She wiggles from a towel and pees on the floor. Mama straps a diaper on. She pages through a book of animals. A panda lies in a casket, surrounded by white flowers. "Died," she says, drawing out the word that has already found her out.

"Just sleeping," Mama says.

"Little bit died," she says.

The two year old cries when Mama wrests the book away. She has warm milk in a sippy cup. She rocks in the chair and cries when placed in the crib. "Mama up," she says. She lays on her back. She turns over. She calms down. "Nigh, nigh," she says as Mama leaves the room.

Through the monitor comes the sound of lively talk. She tells a faceless doll a story about opposites: in and out, on and off, up and down. She lets him know about things that live and things that die. Soon, her voice trails off. There's the static-like sound of shifting back and forth. Then silence.

Downstairs, cleaning up the day, Mama finds the can of olives on the windowsill, the dark orbs on the label still pressed against the pane. She kneels down on the hard wood floor, hand around the can, and studies all that's out there: the tilting pine, the quiet, narrow road, the warm glow of the TV at the home across the way. Time passes, and Mr. Fendrich, retired for years, strides to the curb, garbage can in hand; his grandson, a quiet, well-mannered teen, follows behind with a black pillow of a bag. The chore finished, they gaze at the heavens above. Mr. Fendrich draws intricately in the air before them. He takes his good, sweet time.

It Keeps Going Down

The one thing Donnie loved was a fancy hotel, and when the young blonde in the silver buttoned uniform handed him his key with a coy, "Here you are Mr. Cunningham. Enjoy your stay!" he was on the verge of thinking that all his dreams stood a good chance of coming true.

In the room, Donnie hung his white shirt and sports coat in the closet. He angled the bottle of champagne inside the compact fridge. He turned down the king-sized bed Laura would warm up later on that night. Downstairs, with time to kill before his son arrived, he took a seat in the lobby, enjoying the Christmas tree winking by the front entrance, a family in holiday sweaters drawing complimentary beverages from brass urns, the swift rush of the waterfall behind him. On his left was the bar, dark and lovely even at this time of day. All the years he'd lived in Corning, and he'd never stepped foot in this magnificent—this restful—place. For a moment, Donnie pretended he'd been invited back, the small town guy made good.

Paul was right on time. Donnie hardly recognized his son at first, the shaggy, beard-burdened head swiveling this way and that, a long black coat flapping like a wounded bird. But there was that unmistakable stride, every step an attempt to span a stretch of standing water. As he rose to hail him, Donnie noticed that Paul was not alone. There was a wife or something—a pale little woman in thick frames, stretch pants, and a black beret. Attached to her hand was maybe a three year old boy, his eyes brown triangles of fear.

"You're shitting me," Donnie said, looking down at the boy who shrunk against the leg of the mother.

"Don't swear in front of the child," Paul said.

Donnie couldn't even find his son's mouth amid all that swirling, angry hair.

"Would you, I don't know, like a drink? Celebrate the . . . the new arrival?" Donnie opened his arms, offering the place as his own. "Do You Hear What I Hear" tinkled through a speaker overhead.

"We have quite a bit of shopping to do."

The wife added: "All the best deals are today."

Donnie watched the revolving door spin the three back into the snow, which was falling now as quickly and finely as sand. He had expected some kind of punishment from his son, but not such blunt and final cruelty. After all, he'd been a good father for years—a faithful husband too, unlike any number of his friends. When the money was there, he bought his wife necessary things, took her and Paul on trips up to Seneca Lake and even to the City that one time for the *Phantom* everyone had to see. When the boy wanted to play the viola instead of second base, he said, "You do what you gotta do."

It had been a good life—Donnie would argue "ideal," almost—until one day, out of the blue, his wife began forgetting things she'd just said and done. He took her to see a series of specialists, the last of whom talked not about cures but about slowing things down, seeing a counselor, preparing for the inevitable. He also said, "never underestimate the power of prayer," and Donnie almost punched him in the face.

At home, fresh from the diagnosis, his wife put the kettle on for coffee. She dropped two spoons of sugar into his mug, proud to have remembered that was just what he liked. Then, clearing her throat, she asked quietly for a divorce.

"Are you?—" he stammered. "Do you think I could?—"

Donnie's wife stopped him with a hand. There was no way on earth she was going to put her loved ones through something like this.

"Send Paul money," she said. "When the time comes, Cynthia will know what to do." That was the extent of her plan.

The kettle breathed over blue fire. It ticked and knocked and came to boil.

His wife folded her hands. Her eyes were tearless and calm, and Donnie wondered if she'd already forgotten what she'd said. The kettle whistled, and he put fingers to his mouth—bars that certain words would soon begin to bend.

Days later, after the shock wore off, he began to consider the plan. A few years earlier, Cynthia—the born again sister, the happy-go-lucky martyr—had taken their mother home to die. When the time came, she'd gladly take in Paul, make sure he finished high school. Donnie could have done this, he supposed, but women were, as a rule, much better with children. And besides, hadn't he been in Paul's life long enough to make his mark? Yes, sure—the more he thought about it, the more there seemed to be a sense to it all. But for the long winter weeks that followed, the plan remained a wild fantasy, preposterous as science fiction.

One Friday afternoon, his shift at the glass factory done, Donnie found himself creeping past the bar where he'd meet his buddies for a beer or two. He turned onto Route 17 and drove the speed limit all the way to Binghamton. In a fast food restaurant, he blew on coffee. He sipped it, some more and some more, and when it was gone the empty cup was like a confirmation. He drove out of the lot and, veering into the fast lane, plunged down, down, down to the Jersey shore, where an old acquaintance from his construction days had more work than he could handle. Once settled, he only called his wife to say the necessary papers were on the way. He never wrote, other than to send checks to Paul for the undergraduate degree he'd never even finish. Some of the checks were cashed, others were not. Donnie, a new life unfolding, decided not to think about what that might mean.

So why start doing so now? Shaking off the nonsense with his son, Donnie headed to the bar for a gin and tonic.

When the drink was placed in front of him, he was sad for a moment to see how clear it was, how simple and ineffectual. He tested it with a long, steady drink. Not bad; in time, it might do the job. A newspaper was in pieces at his left, and he picked up each section for awhile: foreclosure and gang fighting throughout the dreary front pages; East over Watkins Glen in the Tip-Off Tourney; venison recipes just in time for deer season, which made him think of the annual outing with Al Lawton, who was probably gutting a buck as Donnie sat here with his drink. Half-heartedly, he paged through the Classifieds long enough to know there were no jobs here either.

Donnie ordered another and checked his watch. Laura wouldn't finish her shift for another hour. And then, of course, she'd have to shower and slip on that nice dress he'd sent the previous week. As fastidious as she was, she might not arrive for another two hours or more. Donnie hadn't come to see his son, but the shorter-than-expected interview left him with a giant hole in the itinerary.

"Another?" the barmaid asked.

"Please," he said cheerily. He was going to make a real effort to enjoy the luxury for which he paid.

A college football game was ending on the plasma screen above. A coach stood over a petite woman with a microphone.

"The kids out there . . . I can't say enough . . ." The coach rubbed his forehead with a palm. "We just ran out of time."

The barmaid laughed. "What were they going to do with

more time? Toss another pick?"

Donnie shrugged.

"They lost, am I right? I don't know much about this dumb game, but 28 beats 23 every single time."

"That's that Avery creep," an old man at the end of the bar explained. A white, sloppily applied patch on his cheek made him look like a pirate who missed the point.

"Brainless asshole ruined the program at Illinois—they're on probation now. It won't be long—"

Donnie shifted on the bar stool. It was true he had not made *all* the possible sacrifices his wife's illness had called for, but he did give up an excellent job. He'd been at the Glassworks since '73, had four weeks of vacation, health insurance, and a benefits package second to none. He'd given up status. For years, when he strode down Market for the Fourth of July parade, people—total strangers—would slip off the curb with eager, flag waving kids to thank him for his service. He'd given up his only child, the smart, awkward kid who turned into a beast with terrible hair. And his grandson too, the fearful boy who would remember him (if at all) as some shellshocked fool in a fancy hotel lobby. Donnie ground his teeth against a chunk of ice. If he'd gotten away with anything, it certainly hadn't been much.

"Charge it to your room?" the barmaid asked.

"No, no," he said. "I've got cash." He fumbled in his wallet, tossed two bills onto the bar and added a third just to hear the barmaid cry "oh!"

Donnie left, buoyed by his beneficence. At the elevator, though, all his enthusiasm leaked away. Eyes closed, he leaned against a wall of the box that lifted him to the second floor. The corridor was silent, filled with identical doors. The door to the room next to his was open, a vacuum like a sentry standing out front. He peeked in just as the housekeeper was drawing the blinds, an act that made him remember his wife on their honeymoon at Niagara Falls. He'd ordered room service, expensive as hell, and was somewhere between elation and regret when she awakened from a nap.

They sat out on the balcony to watch water plunge and foam like champagne from a bottle. "It keeps going down," Donnie observed. She said, "No kidding," hair blowing across her smiling lips, her child-sleepy eyes. It was the moment she should have been lovely, but something about her had just missed the mark. Suddenly, he wondered: What was he doing with this woman? What was he doing in this kind of life? He smiled bravely, a white fib of the lips.

The memory tactfully refrained from following him into his room. He sat down on the bed, spreading his hands across the comforter. He checked his watch. The phone was stoic in its cradle. Donnie took a deep breath and figured it like this: Laura would arrive and there would be drinks and Filet Mignon at the hotel restaurant; dark, furious lovemaking followed by her appeals to him to move back home already; tears and pillow punching and all the rest; fitful sleep; a breakfast of French toast and forced smiles. Then

Laura, the on-and-off love of his life, would be gone for another six months or more. In fifteen hours or so, Donnie would be right back at the front desk, bag over shoulder, surrendering his key to another bright blonde so she could zap it for the next customer waiting in line. The next moment, he'd be out the door—tired, snow hounded, trying not to dwell on the lives he had left.

"Come here," Wallace said, caressing the cushion beside him.

"No way. And don't touch my sofa."

"I washed. Smell my hands."

"Why weren't you wearing the gloves?"

After dinner, Wallace had gone upstairs to open the bag of chemotherapy pills the Fed-Ex man had delivered earlier in the day. While passing by the study to the bathroom, Martha noticed he was still in his swivel chair, gazing into cupped hands.

"What's wrong?" she asked.

"This one seems to be broken."

She'd read enough of the advisory pamphlet to know to dial the oncologist, asking with wavering voice how dangerous it was to get that "gunk" on one's hands.

"If my stomach can handle it . . ." Wallace said, unable to prevent a smile.

She stepped away, shushed him with a finger to her lips. She asked the nurse to tell her once again that all he needed to do was thoroughly wash and he would be fine.

But now, as Martha studied that hand on the couch, it

seemed like a mutant spider poised to strike. She put a hand over her mouth. He crossed his legs, closed his eyes, tipped his head towards the ceiling. He was the epitome of ease.

"Turn off the lights," she said at last. "Let's at least see what I'm dealing with."

Wallace obliged her. Embarrassed by the absurdity of her request, she stood above him, waiting for his hands to glow. She gazed at his rounded belly, where the first round of treatment was dissolving. She had this image of it, grainy like sand, making indelible scratches along the delicate lining of his veins. Medicine. Poison. With this stuff, there hardly seemed to be a difference. Martha sat down on the edge of the sofa, keeping two full cushions between them.

After a time, Wallace crawled that spider hand her way. She closed her eyes, held her breath, and allowed his fingers to touch. In a month, they'd be married fifty years.

Wallace said, as if reading her mind, "What's a little chemo between dear old friends?"

***

Later, her husband already in bed, Martha took the rest of the day's paper to the front porch swing. As usual, she'd left the front section for last, swallowed it now as if it were one of those clusters of pills and capsules Wallace had to take every single day of his life. There was a car bomb at a funeral in Iraq. In Syria, a child—a boy of thirteen—had been shot dead at a protest, his body mutilated. At home, each political party warned of financial Armageddon. In local news, the state house approved a bill that would allow people to carry guns into bars and restaurants. The measure was supposedly all about self-defense, about keeping up with the laws of other states. Why not airplanes? she thought. Daycare centers? Let's just kill everybody and get it over with.

Not really the Christian point of view, she supposed. But lately, in the last few months or so, the world was starting to become too much for her: the treachery, the dire threats, the pulsing vein of rage. Sometimes—in a flash, here or there—she thought that perhaps God had become nothing more than a deadbeat dad.

Without her husband here to sustain her, she could not even appreciate this uncharacteristically peaceful night in the neighborhood, the cool breeze cooing through the screens. What good was such pleasure if it was only going to pass? Soon enough, tomorrow would be here, the smooth breeze gone, the world further shaken by murder and menace, her very own street cracked open again by screaming kids and roaring cars. Wallace would take more pills, spend hours in one doctor's office or another. The next day, more of the same. And yet, and yet—for all the world's turbulence, there was still the gift of time. The problem was: How much time? Certainly not more than there'd been a day before.

Martha had a thyroid issue a few years ago, and her choles-terol was higher than the doctor liked, but, all things considered, she was in excellent health. Wallace, on the other hand, was an encyclopedia of ailments: high blood pressure, arthritis, a weak heart, an enlarged prostate, diabetes, and now this awful cancer of the skin. Her husband was, to put it frankly, in a bad way, yet this plague of old age was all still a game for him, or, at worst, a puzzle he'd figure out before too long. She wanted to know: What exactly was his problem?

Next door, there was a sudden bang, the primal wail of an infant. Then the new people were at it again—the woman first, voice teetering between rage and desperation, then the man, whose scream exploded from the open window. Martha half expected a rain of molten debris.

In recent years, the houses around them had been transformed into rentals. Young, tenuously attached couples with loud cars and voices moved in. They kept apoplectic dogs behind short and feeble chain linked fences. Inevitably, there were children—lots of them: screamers, faces smudged with dirt and runny food, clothes too small or big for them. Martha tried like her husband to be neighborly—learn names, shoot the breeze, sit on another porch, speak an encouraging word or two to screaming kids firing by on their bikes—but everyone seemed so angry and aimless to her. Young as they were, and scantily schooled, this new generation of parents seemed to intuit that life had given them the shaft. The compensation? Like kids with parents gone for the weekend, they could do whatever it was they wanted.

A black SUV swung into the driveway next door, horn bleating, music like an earthquake behind its windows. The door to the house flew open, and the man bounded down the stairs, buttoning his shirt.

"You're the sick one," he said, turning around at the woman who surged to the stairs, dressed in nothing but a tank top and a pair of flabby underwear.

"I work! I deserve *my* drinks!" she cried, following up with a string of expletives that made Martha wince.

The SUV backed out, screeched off, and the woman, suddenly drained, shuffled quietly back into the house. A few moments later, a child—this one, a fat girl of five or six—stepped outside, leaned against the railing facing Martha's house. Out of the corner of her eye, Martha saw the girl walk an unclothed doll across a tight rope of iron.

"Be careful," she said, to say something. "Your baby is going to fall."

"She always falls," the girl said matter-of-factly. She twirled the doll like a top. When the figure pitched forward, the girl caught it against her ample stomach.

Martha picked up the paper again, studied words she already knew. She felt the gaze of the girl upon her, imagined tears welling in her eyes. Why didn't this girl just go to bed? What was she waiting for? Martha was not her mother; she was no one's mother.

Martha stood up, her chest tightening.

"Where are you going?" the girl asked.

Martha clasped the paper to her chest, surprised to think of it now as a long lost friend. "I have to go," she said, unable to look at the child. "I'm going inside now."

***

In bed, Wallace soundly sleeping at her side, Martha couldn't get the girl out of her head. She was mortified, of course, for thinking her "fat" ("Unhealthy" would have been the more charitable term). But didn't she have a right to be angry at those awful parents, who brought home bottle after bottle of soda, bag after bag of chips, all those pre-packaged foods and pizzas whose cartons she saw elbowing out of the garbage bags this past Friday morning. The girl *was* fat, and those bellowing, pit bull like parents were to blame.

Martha had gone into marriage wanting many children; she and Wallace had spent years trying for one. Then, through Wallace's insistence, they applied for the foster boy. Will was his name. The last name G. G something. It shamed her what little she could remember, how infrequently he passed through her mind. A cute boy, that much was certain—full cheeks, omnivorous eyes, a gentle heart. Every night, she made hot, hearty meals in order to put some meat on his bones. He loved Salisbury Steak so much he'd drink the gravy that remained. There were many moments of fun—of pure joy, even—but it wasn't long before Martha was constantly thinking about the day the boy would have to leave.

"Just be patient," Wallace said. "We don't know what's going to happen with the parents."

"Promise me he'll stay."

"Have faith, okay?"

Martha tried to adopt her husband's point of view, but in the evenings, when all was quiet and Will and Wallace were in bed, long shadows of doubt spread out before her. Making things worse was her mother, who'd call once a week to tell Martha things like: "That's no way to have a child," and "Doesn't that husband love you? Doesn't he know how to get things done?"

Martha touched Wallace's bare back, the skin soft as her fingers moved away from the spine. Sick too, of course, but soft as a little boy's face.

***

In the morning, despair clung like sleep breath to Martha's mouth. She sliced fruit and stirred oatmeal with the solemnity of one preparing to dress the dead.

Wallace eased into a chair behind her, said, "Ah, ah, ah, oooh."

"What's wrong?"

"I was trying to sneeze, and forgot how to spell it."

She delivered his food with narrowed eyes.

He shrugged his shoulders, gave her his "what-did-I do?" eyes.

They ate in silence, each with a section of the newspaper. Periodically, he'd chuckle, as if he were reading the comics.

In addition to all those physical ailments and diseases, perhaps Wallace was losing his mind. It had happened to her father, and it wasn't pretty. Those last days—sitting beside his wheelchair in the home, his body limp, face sagging, eyes dead to the world.

She tried to focus on the article in front of her—Hot New Fashions for the Fall! There was a tall, blonde woman on a runway, legs crossed at her heels, her eyes, her expertly painted lips, full of both confidence and challenge. She thought of the child next door, the doll and its high wire act. Only it was Will on that strip of iron, Will smiling and falling with no one to catch him.

"Will!" she said, the name escaping her lips before she'd had the presence of mind to trap it.

Wallace put down the paper, looked her in the eyes. Another husband would have said, "Who?" or "What about him?" or even "Not again!" but Wallace, in a soft voice shorn of humor, simply said, "I know."

Martha, of course, had been right. After six months, Will had to leave them. The mother shaped up, found a job, kicked the boyfriend and the bottle out of her house. She was ready to provide a decent home. Martha could not get rid of the image of the boy in the morning sun, one hand in the social worker's, the other waving to them as they stood hugging on the porch. "I'll see you," he said, his voice bright and reassuring before disappearing into the car.

Wallace was still looking at her, eyes soft and patient. In

a vague way, he reminded her of her father, in those tender days before his mind was gone for good.

"It's not going to end well," she said, gazing at the plate of sliced strawberries like vibrant hearts between them.

"What isn't?"

She threw up her hands to indicate the room, the house, the oatmeal, their long, long life together.

"Nothing ends well," he said, reaching out a hand for hers. "But the end . . . Isn't it such a little part of the whole big thing?"

How often in fifty years had Wallace made her want to scream? Now, though, it was crying that gave Martha more of what she was looking for.

Other Side of the Bed

We marry. Simple enough. First night, she takes the left side, I take the right. It works. We go to Cedar Point, Niagara Falls. We visit her sister in Detroit. Same thing: left side, right side. I work on an assembly line.

I never thought that thirty years could happen. It does. She's in the Cleveland Clinic. Our first night apart. Her side is big and interesting now. There are tiny lumps in the sheets where she was last night. I move across the mattress. Over the side is something: Magazines. Make up. Face cream. Loose change. A man. Yes, a man. Can you believe it? He's good-looking, I give him that. Big chin, square shoulders, thick head of hair.

OK, good-looking man, tell me who you are. I'll wait three seconds before I get the gun.

I love your wife, he says. We've met everyday for the last twenty years on the other side of this bed. He shrugs his shoulders. You were a sound sleeper.

You're kidding me. Is this a joke? What else is there?

A door. He opens it and I'm in a small apartment. It looks nothing like our home. He leads me down a hallway with pictures.

Those are hers.

We don't have that kind of money.

She painted them herself.

They're swirls, as far as I can tell. Everything runs together. I don't see any bodies, any thing that looks like the things outside the window.

The good-looking man shows me the bedroom.

We sleep at angles, he says. She calls this intimacy.

He tells me these things. To my face. Can you believe it?

Look old man, look in here, and he takes out a book with flowers on it. Pretty. Her writing inside. I've never seen it. Folded up is a letter saying I loved you but I never loved you. I thought the years would be like sheets I'd peel away, and after ten, fifteen, or twenty there'd be some warm, throbbing bed of love.

I know about work, American cars, telling Jack to go to his room so many years ago. We go on vacation, I get us there. What do I know about women?

The man puts his hand on my shoulder, says meet me down the street for a good, stiff drink? What the hell. Dorothy may die of cancer, I should be drinking. We close the door, and I step back into our room, look at our bed. It's bigger now—an island without people. I open my wallet, read my license from top to bottom. This is my life, alright.

Down on Pearl Road, there's a neon sign saying Onley's, a bunch of men like me. Old, hands in pockets, stomachs round like shirts over heads. The good-looking lover is there, holding the door, sweeping his hand inside. A hundred guys walk into a bar. Can you believe it? It's the beginning of the world's longest joke. Where's the punch line? Go home and see for yourself.

A Little Piece

If I get better—

Please don't use that word.

I'd like to rent down here. A place we could stay for a month or two. You know, live a different kind of life for once.

Are you hungry yet?

How come we never made it sooner?

Andrew, are you hungry?

Not really.

You sure?

I think so.

How about a little something?

What do you have?

Corned beef.

My favorite.

Well?

Why don't you just set it out there.

She looked at him. Her long fingers curled on the towel.

I could very well be hungry in a little while.

She reached into the cooler, set the sandwich down on the towel. She folded back the foil, pressing it flat as possible.

Both studied the thick slices of meat, the hearty whole wheat bread. They looked like they were expecting the sandwich to get up and walk. Maybe feed the masses.

I'm almost hungry. Any minute now.

She smiled.

Hunger looms.

She laughed a little. She wiped her eyes.

He anchored his toes in the sand.

What are you doing?

He reached for the sandwich, plucked a tiny piece of fat. It hung limp from his fingers, like a flag on a hot, still day of surrender.

CREDITS

"Worse Things" was previously published in *Pindeldyboz* (June 19, 2005).

"All I Am Is Nine" was previous published in *Tattoo Highway* (Summer 2004).

"Squeeze" was previously published in *Whistling Shade* (Winter 2003-2004).

"Late for Play" was previously published in *Slow Trains* (Fall 2007).

"Brother and Sister and Love" was previously published in *Galleon* (Summer 2008).

"Someday Morning" was previously published in *Slow Trains* (Spring 2003).

"Whack" was previously published in *Atticus Review* (December 13, 2011).

"Retroactive Special" was previously published in *Stickman Review* (December 2006).

"Air" was previously published in *Peeks and Valleys* (October 2005).

"Ladies" was previously published in *HiNgE* 5.1 (Spring 2004).

"Third Anniversary" was previously published in *971 Menu* (August 2007).

"Execution Style" was previously published in *Newport Review* (Summer 2008).

"Left Only" was previously published in *Thunder Sandwich #21*

(Summer 2003).

"Exquisite Alarm" was previously published in *Flashquake* (Winter 2005-2006).

"Bounce the Ball" was previously published in *Eclectica Magazine* (Oct./Nov. 2003).

"August Is Young" was previously published in *Snow Monkey* (June 2004).

"God She Could Tolerate" was previously published in *Relief* (Winter 2011).

"The Please Pitch" was previously published in *Monday Night* (2006).

"Everything Off" was previously published in *Dirty Napkin* (March 2008).

"Opposites" was previously published in *Staccato Fiction* (Spring 2010).

"It Keeps Going Down" was previously published in *SNReview* (Winter/Spring 2011)

"Other Side of the Bed" was previously published in *Stray Dog* (Winter 2004).

"A Little Piece" was previously published in *Staccato Fiction* (Spring 2011).

Fomite
Burlington, Vermont

Fomite is a literary press whose authors and artists explore the human condition -- political, cultural, personal and historical -- in poetry and prose.

A fomite is a medium capable of transmitting infectious organisms from one individual to another.

"The activity of art is based on the capacity of people to be infected by the feelings of others." Tolstoy, *What is Art?*

AlphaBetaBestiario - Antonello Borra
Animals have always understood that mankind is not fully at home in the world. Bestiaries, hoping to teach, send out warnings. This one, of course, aims at doing the same.

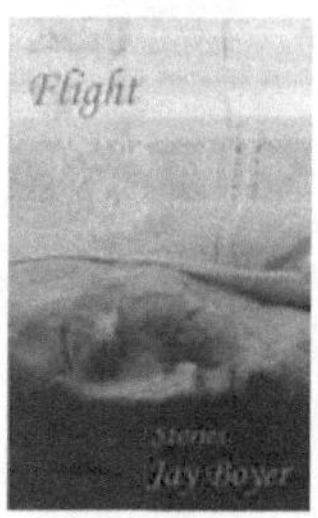

Flight and Other Stories - Jay Boyer
In *Flight and Other Stories,* we're with the fattest woman on earth as she draws her last breaths and her soul ascends toward its final reward. We meet a divorcee who can fly for no more effort than flapping her arms. We follow a middle-aged butler whose love affair with a young woman leads him first to the mysteries of bondage, and then to the pleasures of malice. Story by story, we set foot into worlds so strange as to seem all but surreal, yet everything feels familiar, each moment rings true. And that's when we recognize we're in the hands of one of America's truly original talents.

Improvisational Arguments - Anna Faktorovich
Improvisational Arguments is written in free verse to capture the essence of modern problems and triumphs. The poems clearly relate short, frequently humorous and occasionally tragic, stories about travels to exotic and unusual places, fantastic realms, abnormal jobs, artistic innovations, political objections, and misadventures with love.

Fomite
Burlington, Vermont

Loisaida - Dan Chodorokoff

Catherine, a young anarchist estranged from her parents and squatting in an abandoned building on New York's Lower East Side is fighting with her boyfriend and conflicted about her work on an underground newspaper. After learning of a developer's plans to demolish a community garden, Catherine builds an alliance with a group of Puerto Rican community activists. Together they confront the confluence of politics, money, and real estate that rule Manhattan. All the while she learns important lessons from her great-grandmother's life in the Yiddish anarchist movement that flourished on the Lower East Side at the turn of the century. In this coming of age story, family saga, and tale of urban politics, Dan Chodorkoff explores the "principle of hope", and examines how memory and imagination inform social change.

Still Time - Michael Cocchiarale

Still Time is a collection of twenty-five short and shorter stories exploring tensions that arise in a variety of contemporary relationships: a young boy must deal with the wrath of his out-of-work father; a woman runs into a man twenty years after an awkward sexual encounter; a wife, unable to conceive, imagines her own murder, as well as the reaction of her emotionally distant husband; a soon-to-be tenured English professor tries to come to terms with her husband's shocking return to the religion of his youth; an assembly line worker, married for thirty years, discovers the surprising secret life of his recently hospitalized wife. Whether a few hundred or a few thousand words, these and other stories in the collection depict characters at moments of deep crisis. Some feel powerless, overwhelmed—unable to do much to change the course of their lives. Others rise to the occasion and, for better or for worse, say or do the thing that might transform them for good. Even in stories with the most troubling of endings, there remains the possibility of redemption. For each of the characters, there is still time.

Loosestrife - Greg Delanty

This book is a chronicle of complicity in our modern lives, a witnessing of war and the destruction of our planet. It is also an attempt to adjust the more destructive blueprint myths of our society. Often our cultural memory tells us to keep quiet about the aspects that are most challenging to our ethics, to forget the violations we feel and tremors that keep us distant and numb.

Fomite
Burlington, Vermont

Carts and Other Stories - Zdravka Evtimova
Roots and wings are the key words that best describe the short story collection, *Carts and Other Stories,* by Zdravka Evtimova. The book is emotionally multilayered and memorable because of its internal power, vitality and ability to touch both the heart and your mind. Within its pages, the reader discovers new perspectives true wealth, and learns to see the world with different eyes. The collection lives on the borders of different cultures. *Carts and Other Stories* will take the reader to wild and powerful Bulgarian mountains, to silver rains in Brussels, to German quiet winter streets and to wind bitten crags in Afghanistan. This book lives for those seeking to discover the beauty of the world around them, and will have them appreciating what they have— and perhaps what they have lost as well.

The Listener Aspires to the Condition of Music - Barry Goldensohn
"I know of no other selected poems that selects on one theme, but this one does, charting Goldensohn's career-long attraction to music's performance, consolations and its august, thrilling, scary and clownish charms. Does all art aspire to the condition of music as Pater claimed, exhaling in a swoon toward that one class act? Goldensohn is more aware than the late 19th century of the overtones of such breathing: his poems thoroughly round out those overtones in a poet's lifetime of listening."
John Peck, poet, editor, Fellow of the American Academy of Rome

The Co-Conspirator's Tale - Ron Jacobs

There's a place where love and mistrust are never at peace; where duplicity and deceit are the universal currency. *The Co-Conspirator's Tale* takes place within this nebulous firmament. There are crimes committed by the police in the name of the law. Excess in the name of revolution. The combination leaves death in its wake and the survivors struggling to find justice in a San Francisco Bay Area noir by the author of the underground classic *The Way the Wind Blew:A History of the Weather Underground* and the novel *Short Order Frame Up*.

Fomite
Burlington, Vermont

When You Remember Deir Yassin - R.L Green
When You Remember Deir Yassin is a collection of poems by R. L. Green, an American Jewish writer, on the subject of the occupation and destruction of Palestine. Green comments: "Outspoken Jewish critics of Israeli crimes against humanity have, strangely, been called "anti-Semitic" as well as the hilariously illogical epithet "self-hating Jews." As a Jewish critic of the Israeli government, I have come to accept these accusations as a stamp of approval and a badge of honor, signifying my own fealty to a central element of Jewish identity and ethics: one must be a lover of truth and a friend to the oppressed, and stand with the victims of tyranny, not with the tyrants, despite tribal loyalty or self-advancement. These poems were written as expressions of outrage, and of grief, and to encourage my sisters and brothers of every cultural or national grouping to speak out against injustice, to try to save Palestine, and in so doing, to reclaim for myself my own place as part of the Jewish people." The poems are offered in the original English with Arabic and Hebrew translations accompanying each poem.

Kasper Planet: Comix and Tragix - Peter Schumann
The British call him Punch, the Italians, Pulchinello, the Russians, Petruchka, the Native Americans, Coyote. These are the figures we may know. But every culture that worships authority will breed a Punch-like, anti-authoritan resister. Yin and yang -- it has to happen. The Germans call him Kasper. Truth-telling and serious pranking are dangerous professions when going up against power. Bradley Manning sits naked in solitary; Julian Assange is pursued by Interpol, Obama's Department of Justice, and Amazon.com. But -- in contrast to merely human faces -- masks and theater can often slip through the bars. Consider our American Kaspers: Charlie Chaplin, Woody Guthrie, Abby Hoffman, the Yes Men -- theater people all, utilizing various forms to seed critique. Their profiles and tactics have evolved along with those of their enemies. Who are the bad guys that call forth the Kaspers? Over the last half century, with his Bread & Puppet Theater, Peter Schumann has been tireless in naming them, excoriating them with Kasperdom....
from Marc Estrin's Foreword to Planet Kasper

Fomite
Burlington, Vermont

Roadworthy Creature, Roadworthy Craft

- Kate Magill

Words fail but the voice struggles on. The culmination of a decade's worth of performance poetry, *Roadworthy Creature, Roadworthy Craft* is Kate Magill's first full-length publication. In lines that are sinewy yet delicate, Magill's poems explore the terrain where idea and action meet, where bodies and words commingle to form a strange new flesh, a breathing text, an "I" that spirals outward from itself.

Zinsky the Obscure - Ilan Mochari

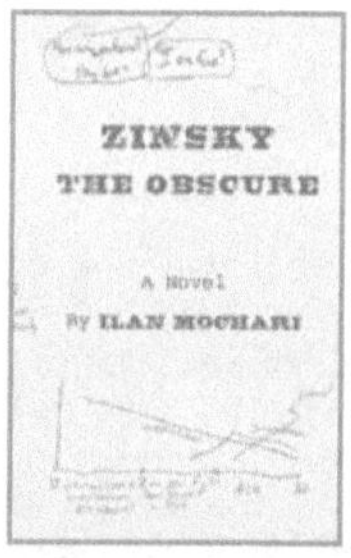

"If your childhood is brutal, your adulthood becomes a daily attempt to recover: a quest for ecstasy and stability in recompense for their early absence." So states the 30-year-old Ariel Zinsky, whose bachelor-like lifestyle belies the torturous youth he is still coming to grips with. As a boy, he struggles with the beatings themselves; as a grownup, he struggles with the world's indifference to them. *Zinsky the Obscure* is his life story, a humorous chronicle of his search for a redemptive ecstasy through sex, an entrepreneurial sports obsession, and finally, the cathartic exercise of writing it all down. Fervently recounting both the comic delights and the frightening horrors of a life in which he feels – always – that he is not like all the rest, Zinsky survives the worst and relishes the best with idiosyncratic style, as his heartbreak turns into self-awareness and his suicidal ideation into self-regard. A vivid evocation of the all-consuming nature of lust and ambition – and the forces that drive them.

Views Cost Extra - *L.E. Smith*

Views that inspire, that calm, or that terrify – all come at some cost to the viewer. In *Views Cost Extra* you will find a New Jersey high school preppy who wants to inhabit the "perfect" cowboy movie, a rural mailman disgusted with the residents of his town who wants to live with the penguins, an ailing screen writer who strikes a deal with Johnny Cash to reverse an old man's failures, an old man who ponders a young man's suicide attempt, a one-armed blind blues singer who wants to reunite with the car that took her arm on the assembly line -- and more. These stories suggest that we must pay something to live even ordinary lives.

Fomite
Burlington, Vermont

The Derivation of Cowboys & Indians
- Joseph D. Reich

The Derivation of Cowboys & Indians represents a profound journey, a breakdown of The American Dream from a social, cultural, historical, and spiritual point of view. Reich examines in concise!detail the loss of the collective unconscious, commenting on our! contemporary postmodern culture with its self-interested excesses, on where and how things all go wrong, and how social/political practice rarely meets its original proclamations and promises. Reich's surreal and self-effacing satire brings this troubling message home. *The Derivations of Cowboys & Indians* is a desperate search and struggle for America's literal, symbolic, and spiritual home.

The Empty Notebook Interrogates Itself

- Susan Thomas

The Empty Notebook began its life as a very literal metaphor for a few weeks of what the poet thought was writer's block, but was really the struggle of an eccentric persona to take over her working life. It won. And for the next three years everything she wrote came to her in the voice of the Empty Notebook, who, as the notebook began to fill itself, became rather opinionated, changed gender, alternately acted as bully and victim, had many bizarre adventures in exotic locales and developed a somewhat politically-incorrect attitude. It then began to steal the voices and forms of other poets and tried to immortalize itself in various poetry reviews. It is now thrilled to collect itself in one slim volume.

Fomite
Burlington, Vermont

My God, What Have We Done? - Susan Weiss

In a world afflicted with war, toxicity, and hunger, does what we do in our private lives really matter? Fifty years after the creation of the atomic bomb at Los Alamos, newlyweds Pauline and Clifford visit that once-secret city on their honeymoon, compelled by Pauline's fascination with Oppenheimer, the soulful scientist. The two stories emerging from this visit reverberate back and forth between the loneliness of a new mother at home in Boston and the isolation of an entire community dedicated to the development of the bomb. While Pauline struggles with unforeseen challenges of family life, Oppenheimer and his crew reckon with forces beyond all imagining.

Finally the years of frantic research on the bomb culminate in a stunning test explosion that echoes a rupture in the couple's marriage. Against the backdrop of a civilization that's out of control, Pauline begins to understand the complex, potentially explosive physics of personal relationships.

At once funny and dead serious, *My God, What Have We Done?* sifts through the ruins left by the bomb in search of a more worthy human achievement.